"Colleges! Exams! We're all going a little crazy. Do you remember when we thought all there was to senior year was getting to sit around the senior fountain?" Sam said.

"If senior year were a car, it would be recalled."

Luke grinned. "If it were a rock star, it would look like Alice Cooper."

"If it were a note, it would be flat."

"If it were a cat, it would be pregnant."

"If it were a boyfriend," said Sam, "it would be working on its senior thesis."

Books by Janice Harrell

Puppy Love
Heavens to Bitsy
Secrets in the Garden
Killebrew's Daughter
Sugar 'n' Spice
Blue Skies and Lollipops
Birds of a Feather
With Love from Rome
Castles in Spain
A Risky Business
Starring Susy
They're Rioting in Room 32
Love and Pizza to Go
B.J. on Her Own
Masquerade
The Gang's All Here
Dear Dr. Heartbreak
Your Daily Horoscope
So Long, Senior Year

JANICE HARRELL earned her M.A. and Ph.D. from the University of Florida, and for a number of years taught English on the college level. She is the author of a number of books for teens, as well as a mystery novel for adults. She lives in North Carolina.

JANICE HARRELL

So Long, Senior Year

Keepsake

FROM
CROSSWINDS

CROSSWINDS

New York • Toronto • Sydney
Auckland • Manila

First publication December 1988

ISBN 0-373-88038-3

Printed in the U.S.A.

RL 6.2, IL age 12 and up

Dear Reader:

Welcome to our line of teen romances, Keepsake from *CROSSWINDS*. Here, as you can see, the focus is on the relationship between girls and boys, while the setting, story and the characters themselves contribute the variety and excitement you demand.

As always, your comments and suggestions are welcome.

The Editors
CROSSWINDS

Chapter One

Pip's mother lay stretched out on the sofa, her long legs swathed in afghans and the Fenterville *Banner* spread over her stomach. "I feel awful," she whimpered. "Don't come near me. You'll catch it. Tell Cassandra to bring me some hot tea, will you?" Convulsed by a sneeze, she groped helplessly for a tissue, her eyes streaming.

When Pip returned from the kitchen with the tray of tea, his mother was cutting something out of the paper. Later it seemed to him that all the most traumatic events of his senior year left their trail in those newspaper clippings his mother collected. Just then she was snipping out a picture of Pip, Marcy McNair and Lutisha Davis standing stiffly shoulder-to-shoulder, their faces reduced to vague pale shapes— "Morehead Nominees Announced."

After wiping her nose, Pip's mother swabbed some glue on the clipping and slapped it firmly into her scrapbook. When it came to newspaper stories about the family, she had no discrimination. The picture of Pip's second-grade class's rhythm band was in her scrapbook next to the press snapshot of his father's totaled Porsche, a reminder of a close call they all shuddered to remember. Pip couldn't understand why she wanted a clipping like that. It was some perverted magpie instinct at work. And now that Pip's father was beginning to mount a campaign for governor there would be an avalanche of clippings. Phillip Byron speaks to Rotary Club, Phillip Byron Consults with Civic Leaders. Pip wondered if she had ever heard of subscribing to a clipping service. He decided not to mention it. He didn't want to encourage her.

"If you're sick," he said, "I'd better call Sam and tell her."

His mother clutched her head with both hands. "Oh, dough! I forgot. She was coming over for dinner, wasn't she? Let's make it next week instead. I ought to be okay by then." She blew her nose and added darkly, "If I survive, that is."

"I think I'll take her out for dinner."

"That's a good idea." Pip's mother put the scrapbook on the coffee table and leaned back once more on the couch, touching the tissue gingerly to her raw-looking nose. "I can't believe a cold would do this to me. Maybe it's pneumonia." She thumped on her chest with her fist as if expecting a confirmation of her diagnosis.

Pip picked up the scrapbook and looked at the clipping. As bad as the photograph was, it still conveyed something of the animosity Marcy had directed toward him that day. It was there in the inflection of her head and the way her body seemed to cringe away from him. "Look at that," he said glumly. "If looks could kill, I'd be dead meat. I can't figure out why Marcy hates me. I've never done anything to her."

"You keep on expecting people to be reasonable," said his mother. "You're like your father that way."

Pip closed the scrapbook. "I'm going to go call Sam. You want me to get you anything first?"

She shook her head, then winced and sank back on the pillows holding both hands to her head and uttering a low groan. "Dough," she said. "Just let me die in peace."

That night Pip took Sam to La Petite Marmite, the only decent restaurant in town. Her eyes looked confidingly into his across the table, and her cornsilk-blond hair gleamed in the candlelight. She was wearing something soft and shimmery that sort of clung to her, and it seemed unfair that he couldn't concentrate on her instead of Marcy McNair. He traced a pattern on the tablecloth with his fork.

"Is something wrong?" Sam asked. "Your mother is really sick, isn't she? She isn't just putting me off because she's found out awful things about my character or there's garlic on my breath or something?"

"Nope, she's really sick, all right."

"Then what's wrong? Why are you perforating the tablecloth?"

Self-consciously, Pip put the fork down. "I know this is crazy, but it's kind of getting to me the way Marcy's down on me. I never expected to get really buddy-buddy with your friends, but I kind of hoped for a little basic friendliness by now. That day we got our picture taken for the paper, you should have seen her looking at me. Anybody would have figured I was your average neighborhood ax murderer.''

"She was probably just surprised. She didn't know you were going to be up for the Morehead Scholarship."

"You think that's all it was?"

"Sure."

"I've earned that nomination. I've worked for it. You know that."

"Maybe you'll even win," said Sam, her eyes searching his face.

"Nope. I wanted to be nominated just for the honor of the thing, but the odds are against me winning."

"Marcy could really use that scholarship, Pip. She needs the money. Oh, I wish she would win."

"Don't hold your breath. They don't give out that many."

"If you won you probably wouldn't even use it anyway, would you?"

"Probably not," he admitted. "It's only good at Carolina, and I'll most likely be going out-of-state to school."

Sam stared ahead of her as if what Pip said had dropped between them onto the tablecloth. He saw that her fingers were tightly laced and her knuckles looked white. He had never come right out and said that he planned to go out-of-state to college, though she must have known it. Why else would he have toured all those northeastern campuses with his father? In the long silence that followed he wanted to put his arms around her and comfort her.

"Nobody died," he suggested finally.

"No." Sam slowly lifted her glass and looked at him over it. "Have you made up your mind where you want to go?"

"I thought I'd wait and see where I get accepted first. Yale sounds good to me now. Dad went there. He would like that."

"I guess you want to go to the very best school you can get in."

"Sure. Doesn't everybody?"

"Nope. Some want to stay close to the people they love." She had turned her head and was watching the flames in the fireplace. "Some want to go where they have good parties. Ron Winstead told me that's why he wants to go to Carolina instead of Wake Forest— better parties. A friend of my mother's went to the University of Louisiana because she wanted to be near Mardi Gras, and one of the social workers at my mother's office picked a college solely and exclusively because it offered roller-skating."

"Oh, well," he shrugged. "Flakes."

"Going to a prestige school isn't important to everybody."

"Bet you Marcy doesn't play that tune."

Sam refolded her napkin and put it carefully back on her lap. "No. You two are a lot more alike than you think."

"Ha! Me like Marcy? That's a laugh."

"I don't know what it is with me that I end up with these superachievers," Sam said with a weak smile.

"My best friend, my boyfriend—people must think I'm some kind of secret intellectual."

Pip covered her hand with his own and could feel warmth and peace trickling through him. "People think I'm a lucky guy, that's what they think," he said huskily. "Look, even if I do end up in New Haven, we'd have summers. It's not like I'm going to be nailed to the campus. We can be flying back and forth all the time."

"If we like," Sam agreed. "Of course, we'll be meeting all sorts of new people at college, too. That's part of the whole point of going away to school. Broader horizons and all that."

Pip sensed that Sam had drawn away from him a little, and he was conscious of a miserably familiar stirring of sick jealousy. After all, Sam was so warm and lovely it was likely she would meet a lot more new people than he would. He remembered how she liked to dance and wished it weren't so easy to imagine her dancing with other guys. She was usually good about reassuring him. If only she would say something to reassure him now. He wanted her to say that she would always love him, that she would wait for him, that she wouldn't even consider going out with anybody else. Empty promises when people are going off in two different directions, maybe, but he would have liked to hear them just the same.

The waiter appeared and asked solicitously about the food. When he had gone, Sam took a deep breath. "I think you should go to one of those hotshot schools in the East, Pip. That's right for you, and I don't mean to make you feel bad about it."

"You can't make me feel worse about it than I feel already. I know there are going to be things about being up there that I'm not going to like. I'm sitting here getting selfish and possessive, wishing you were going to some school where the parties weren't quite so great."

"Don't lose sleep over it. Maybe I won't get into Carolina and will have to go to Forest Hills Typing School, where they don't even have parties. It's entirely possible."

"You don't have to go that far to cheer me up. As far as that goes I might not get in where I want to go, either."

"Oh, you'll get in all right."

"I guess I do think I've got a pretty good shot at Yale. And I'd kind of like to see how I'd do when I'm up against some real competition. You know, kids from all over the country. I guess I like competition."

"Maybe because you usually win?"

"Nobody likes to lose."

"I don't think you even know what it's like to lose."

"What are you giving me, Sam? You know better than that. Are you being brainwashed by Marcy or something?"

"I don't know why I said that. I am an idiot. I guess I'm having an anxiety attack or something. All this talk about going away to school. I've never been very good at change. In fact, it was Marcy who pointed that out to me. 'You hate growth and change, Sam,' she said. 'You've still got your first teddy bear.'"

Almost imperceptibly, Pip found himself feeling more cheerful. He realized that all signs of faithfulness in love were welcome, even faithfulness to teddy bears. "No kidding, do you still have your first teddy bear?"

"Absolutely. I'm going to take him to school with me."

Suddenly Pip realized that up till now he had avoided talking about going away as much to protect himself as to protect Sam. He didn't like to think about what the separation might mean. The whole idea of Sam going out with other guys made him feel vaguely sick to his stomach.

He had always known he would go up north to school. It had been implicitly understood in his family that it would be healthier for him to get a taste of the world beyond North Carolina instead of spending his entire life in the shadow of his family's tobacco company. There was no denying that people around here treated him differently when they found out who he was. It would be good to get away from all that. If he did eventually come back to take his place in the company, as his father had before him, it would be only after a career of his own in some other field. That was what his parents had in mind for him, and Pip had no quarrel with the plan. What he had not counted on was that when it came to the point of leaving, his fear of losing Sam would pull on him like a brake.

Chapter Two

I've always been nice to him for your sake, Sam," Marcy said, as she paced the floor of Sam's bedroom. "Okay, well, maybe not exactly *nice*, but I've never been actually mean to him. It's just that I practically dropped my teeth when it turned out he was a Morehead nominee, that's all. I ask you, is it fair? His daddy's rich and his mammy's good-looking, and he gets a shot at the Morehead on top of it? Where's the justice in it?"

"There is no justice," said Sam. "I thought you knew that. Marce, I think Pip's going to go to Yale."

Marce threw her hands in the air. "That figures, right? I mean, he's got a Mercedes, and now he gets Yale, too. *He* doesn't need any scholarship. I suppose they'll send him up to school in a private Lear jet tended by houris who pop peeled grapes in his mouth the whole way. Do you happen to know what his SATs were? No, don't tell me. I don't want to know. I truly do not."

"Why don't you try taking a few deep breaths and counting to ten," said Sam. "I think you're coming unglued."

"Okay, so I'm coming unglued. I've got every excuse. You know, all this stuff about how seniors don't have much to do, they just coast along and enjoy themselves—it's a myth. They were stringing us along. When I close my eyes this interminable essay starts rolling past on my eyelids, like on a player piano— 'Why I Want to Attend Yawknapatawfa University and What I Think I Could Contribute.' I've written three of them—one for my first-choice school, one for my second-choice and an abbreviated version for Disasterville U." Marcy threw herself down on Sam's bed in a posture of discouragement. "Sam, why didn't you tell me that Pip was going to be a Morehead nominee? You had to know about it."

"I did have an idea he might be. But I couldn't think of a good time to mention it. Somehow I had this feeling it wouldn't cheer you up. He doesn't think he's going to win, though."

"Probably none of us are going to win. That's not the point. The point is, I didn't even realize Pip was in the running. I didn't know he had the grades. I hate to ask, but what kind of grades does he have exactly?"

Sam rubbed her nose uncomfortably. "Dad told me he's right behind you in the class standing."

Marcy let out a faint moan and grabbed at a pillow. "How do you think it makes me feel to have Pip Byron breathing down my neck? Do you realize this means we're going to be up on the platform at graduation together? Lovers of symmetry will adore it—the valedictorian and salutatorian, the prince and the pauper.''

"Oh, come on, Marcy."

Under her dark bangs, Marcy's eyes narrowed until only her irises showed, glittering with suspicion. "I wonder exactly what his average is? He didn't transfer in until his junior year—I wonder how they handled his grades from that private school he used to go to."

"Why are you so *down* on Pip?" Sam cried.

Marcy looked at her in surprise. "I'm not down on him, Sam."

"You hurt his feelings. He's a human being, you know. Sometimes you act as if he's some kind of subsidiary of Byron Tobacco Company or something."

Marcy thought about that a minute. She had always valued Sam's powers of empathy. Back in the fourth grade when everybody had called her Marcy the Brain, Sam had been able to see the person behind the high grades and had been her good friend. Evidently Sam could also see behind the Byron money and could get fond of Pip. It was a virtue, all right, and Marcy's own inability to do the same made her suddenly feel shabby and small.

"I'm afraid of him, Sam," she said softly.

"Afraid of Pip?"

"He's got all that money and power and family behind him, and all I've got is me."

"We're all afraid. It's this senior-year stuff. I'm going slightly bats myself."

"I thought you told me your parents had already saved just about enough to send you to Carolina. What can you be worried about?"

"I already told you. Pip is going away to college. And I mean *really* away."

"Well, what did you expect?"

"I was hoping he would go to Carolina or maybe Duke. Okay, maybe I didn't exactly expect it, but I still hoped. I'm afraid he's going to go up north and meet all these glamorous, intellectual Yankee girls who buy their clothes in New York and who are always reading about, oh, intellectual things when they aren't being sexy and sleeping around!" she wailed.

Marcy laughed. "I'm sorry, Sam. But you do make it sound funny."

"At least I know I'll survive. That's one thing I learned when Pip and I broke up that time."

"You were apart one week, weren't you? An eternity. Oops! Wait a minute, for a second there I forgot I was supposed to be comforting you."

"Okay, maybe it wasn't for long and maybe I was miserable the whole time, but the point is I didn't actually end up in a straitjacket."

"You are strong, Sam! You are independent. Besides, think of all those incredible guys you'll meet at Carolina."

"I could get a bigger kick out of that if I were sure Pip would be waiting after the party was over."

"Life isn't like that. No guarantees."

"I know," said Sam. "That's what I'm afraid of." Marcy noticed that Sam had unconsciously begun stroking the head of her teddy bear.

The door to the bedroom burst open. "Greetings, earthlings," said Luke. He threw himself on the bed.

"Ouch," said Sam. "You're lying on my leg."

Luke agreeably shifted his position. "Your mother said I could come right up."

Sam slid awkwardly around him and stood up. "I don't think this is exactly what Mom had in mind. But since you're here, you can give Marcy a ride home."

"My car wouldn't start," Marcy explained. "Sam had to come get me."

"So you're giving us the old heave-ho, Sam? Throwing us out? Can this be? No time for your friends anymore? Casting us off like old shoes, forgotten, neglected. Heck, I thought maybe Marcy and me could stay here awhile and make out." He put his arm around Marcy and produced a look of exaggerated disappointment. Marcy's heart gave a happy thump. Looking at Luke did that to her sometimes. The white-blond hair falling in softly disordered locks, the blue eyes with their direct, challenging look, the flat stomach and slim flanks squeezed into ragged jeans—they all spelled Luke. In his way he was perfect, though as intensely impractical a love object as white gloves.

She tugged on his shirt. "Take me home. I've got work to do."

"Work, work. All the woman does is work," he complained.

When Luke delivered Marcy home, her mother was still out at her night class. It seemed to Marcy that she could hardly remember when her mother had been home evenings. Sarah McNair was studying to be a

CPA, a career move she hoped would catapult her from the penury of the wages at the teller's window to the relative affluence of the bank's trust department. Marcy only wished her mother had paid more attention to the problem of how to earn a decent living while she was in college when it would have been a lot easier. Instead, in her college days Sarah McNair had been dreamy and impractical. A music major, she had married Marcy's father and in subsequent years had supplemented his meager salary as a music professor by giving clarinet lessons in their home. Their small family had lived happily for years in the Blithe Meadows subdivision with their washer, dryer and secondhand encyclopedia. But then came the divorce—they had turned out not to be so happy after all—and the modest comfort of the Blithe Meadows house had disappeared. Now Marcy and her mother lived in a ratty garage apartment where even paying the electric bill every month was a constant challenge. Marcy knew of kids who had no idea what their family's electric bill was. She only wished she lived in that kind of blissful ignorance.

As Marcy and Luke climbed the steps to the apartment, she was conscious that the paint on the outside was peeling and that the country-style wreath her mother had hung on the door had an air of pitiful bravado. It didn't matter. She could already imagine herself sitting on the shaven lawns of some fine college. She would be smiling, calm and competent, her feet solidly on the first rung of the ladder to success. She would most emphatically not make the mistake of majoring in music.

"You'd better not come in," said Marcy, as she fumbled in her purse for her key.

"Okay," said Luke. "Don't worry. I remember you said you had to get to work." He drew her close up against his quilted jacket and kissed her.

She weakened. "Well, you might like to have a cup of cocoa or something. We could get in out of the cold just for a minute."

"Okay, but don't let me keep you from your work. I wouldn't want to do a rotten thing like that."

Unlike Marcy, Luke rarely brought school books home. He was only interested in doing the minimum of work necessary to ensure he wouldn't have to make up a course in summer school.

Marcy flipped the light switch, and the dark empty apartment was flooded with a pitiless light that seemed to emphasize its shabbiness. The old couch in the living room, which doubled as a bed for her mother, had a coverlet thrown over it to hide the torn place in the upholstery, and over by the space heater the rug had worn down to the bare threads.

In the kitchen a geranium on the sill struggled to produce a bloom. Next to it was an empty milk carton and a blue mug filled with assorted wooden spoons. Marcy tossed the milk carton in the trash, wiped toast crumbs off the counter and pulled out a saucepan for the cocoa.

While she stirred the cocoa, Luke put his arms around her waist. As his lips brushed against the hair on the back of her neck, she shivered. Luke's touch always rocked her and knocked all of the tense thoughts out of her head. She turned to nuzzle his cheek, and he responded by pressing her closer to him. "The cocoa," she murmured.

"Forget the cocoa," he said, and kissed her.

Suddenly there was a hissing sound and the smell of burned milk. Marcy grabbed at the pot and reached for a sponge to wipe up the cocoa that had boiled over around the burner.

She was pouring what was left of the cocoa into cups when she heard her mother come in the front door.

"Enter the chaperone," said Luke. "Stage left."

Marcy heard the thud as an armful of books hit the floor, and shortly her mother appeared at the kitchen door, her face softening in an expression of pleasure. It always disturbed Marcy when her mother shone that warm smile on Luke, maybe because she didn't trust her mother's judgment.

"Cocoa! Great! I don't suppose there's enough for all three of us? It's freezing out there, and I think the car heater has finally kicked the bucket." Marcy's mother peeled off her knit gloves and ran fingers through her dark hair. "I think the thermostat in the classroom must have been turned up to ninety. We sat there baking while Brenner actually left the class to go out and run off some handout sheets. For this we're paying? He's going to do his class preparation on our time?"

Marcy pulled another cup out of the cabinet for her mother.

"All kinds of people told me they'd seen your picture in the paper, hon. I tried to be modest but failed dismally. 'Yes, my daughter the genius,' I said. Be sure to cut out the clipping and send it to your father. He'll

be interested." She picked up one of the cups of cocoa and drifted away to the living room, molting outer
garments as she went.

"Sure," Marcy muttered. "I'll have to send it to
him." Marcy's father had started a new young family
out in Arizona, and she saw no sign that he was interested in her accomplishments. She knew he was busy
trying to feed the three new mouths in his family, but
that didn't make it all right.

"I bet your father won't even recognize you in that
picture," said Luke. "It was so bad I couldn't have
told you from Pip, except that he's taller."

"Luke, did you have any idea that Pip had this high
grade point average that I'm all of a sudden hearing
about?"

He made a face. "Sure. My mother actually read
one of his English papers out loud at the dinner table.
Did she think she was going to inspire me this way, or
what? Actually, all it did was make me want to smash
his face."

"Well, Sam doesn't want to smash his face," said
Marcy, regretfully. "She's as crazy about him as ever.
She seems to have the idea I hurt his feelings by the
way I looked at him or something. Did you ever hear
anything so ridiculous? And you should have heard
her moaning about how he's going away to school,
and that's months and months away."

Luke leaned close to her and touched his nose to
hers. "I can sort of understand that." He put his arms
around her waist. Marcy never looked into Luke's eyes
without being overcome by a longing that was hard to
define. She found herself thinking of distant Italian
skies and of fishing boats sailing free on the open sea.

It took a conscious effort to force her mind back to reality.

She cleared her throat. "Are you still thinking you'll work at the *Banner* next year?"

"Sure. I've already talked to them. I was going to tell you, I talked to Mr. Maxwell, who does the hiring. He knows me because of that summer I worked over there. He says I may have to start out in classified ads, but I've got hopes for beginning with obituaries. I can see it now, my first story—Son Skips College—Mother Kills Self and Spouse."

"Your mother's still pretty upset, huh?"

"Well, think about it. If she hasn't caught on by now that I'm no student, is she ever going to catch on? The answer is she won't. She keeps thinking she'll say the magic word that will turn me on to learning and I'll go toddling off to college with all the good boys and girls."

Marcy congratulated herself that, unlike his parents, she had never made the mistake of trying to change Luke. She saved her energy for where it would do some good, planning a realistic and sensible future for herself. Nothing could change Luke. He was by nature a risk taker who lived by instinct.

"What does your dad say?"

"The usual. Stone silence and red ears. Now and then he stirs himself to make some insightful remark like 'You're just no good.'"

"You seem pretty calm about it. I'm glad you're not letting it get to you."

He shrugged. "I'm used to it. No, I guess that's not true. I never get used to it. In fact, the thing that's really got me worried is that I'm not sure this job at the *Banner* is going to pay enough for me to live away from home. Not even if I have a roommate. Hey, don't look at me in that heartbroken way, okay? It's starting to get me down.''

"I have this slightly crazy thing about money. You know that."

"I know." He looked at her sadly.

"I just worry about you. What will you do if you get sick?"

"I'm never sick."

"What about your car insurance, saving for retirement, things like that. They all cost money, Luke."

"I swear you've got a sixty-five-year-old's brain in an eighteen-year-old's body. It's just too bad we couldn't divide all of that worry of yours up and give half of it to me. That would make my mother a very happy woman, and hey, it wouldn't hurt you to lighten up a little bit, either. Keep in mind that this is just my first job. I'll have others."

Marcy knew that Luke was constitutionally incapable of understanding how important it was to lay a good foundation to your career by going to college. You might as well speak to him in Hottentot.

He gulped down the cocoa. "I'll come over tomorrow afternoon and take a look at the car," he promised.

After he left, Marcy draped an afghan around her shoulders and got in bed. She needed to review for the physics test, but her blood was pulsing through her veins too fast, fueled by worry for Luke. She needed to look at things rationally, as if from a great distance. She decided to write down some of her cooler judgments.

Luke—voted most attractive boy by the senior class, the boyfriend of Marcy (see below). Good-looking, clever, capable of inspiring fierce affection (see asterisk), he has never found it necessary to exert himself for any purpose whatever except to score off people or traditions he despises. It is just possible he is making the ultimate score off of his parents by crowning a dismal academic career with a flat refusal to go to college. Unable to see disaster even when it is looming directly ahead of him, he lives haphazardly from moment to moment, coming in on a wing and a prayer.

Marcy—voted most intelligent girl by the senior class, is nevertheless in love* with Luke (see above). Nothing will divert her from her rationally chosen goal of academic achievement and ultimate financial security, but it must be admitted that she finds Luke a distraction of the highest order. She is afraid he is too busy scoring off his parents to recognize some grim financial realities. When she thinks of him spending his life in some run-down hovel like the one she is now living in, she gets the horrors.

Sam—voted Most Attractive Girl by the senior class. Winning Most Attractive was a great relief to her since she had for months been suffering from the morbid fear she would be voted Most Dependable. She is certainly dependable in the sense of being generally well-organized, sensible and infallibly kind, but she has a slightly ditsy quality. She reads astrology columns and fills her mind with trivia instead of the math formulas and vocabulary items likely to prove useful when taking the SATs. Widely liked, she is the closest friend of Marcy and Luke, and also—God only knows why—the girlfriend of Pip.

Pip—tall, dark, rich, smart and spoiled, he is the only boy in the senior class who drives a Mercedes convertible. He undoubtedly could not tell you what his family's electric bill was if his life depended on it. He is generally quiet and well behaved, but except for that the only thing in his favor is that he has had the good taste to pair off with Sam (see above).

Finding her emotional energy suddenly depleted, Marcy stopped writing. She picked up her physics book instead. Physics was something she dealt with extremely well, even at times like tonight when she was so tired the competing theories about light swam before her eyes.

She looked carefully over the review questions. Probably, she thought, none of the people who envied her grades had any idea of the amount of effort day after day and year after year that went into making good grades. Sometimes she could feel a sour taste rising in her throat when people said, "Oh, of course, you'll do okay on the test, Marcy. You always do." They didn't seem to grasp that she did okay only because of unremitting effort. Nothing could be left to chance. Physics was easy for her, but she would never have thought of skating through tomorrow's test on the strength of her aptitude for it. Tired as she was, she went over the entire unit, making sure she could count on total recall.

When she had finally assured herself that Mr. Purcell's questions could hold no surprises for her, she sagged against the headboard of the bed and doodled at the bottom of the page of her notebook—*Luke, Luke, Luke.* She drew a fat heart around his name. "I have loved you so long," she thought, "delighting in your company." That was a line from "Greensleeves" and it described to a T the way she felt. She and Luke had been friends since they were kids. However far away she went, however long she stayed away, she would still care about what happened to him. She wasn't sure that was an unmixed blessing.

Chapter Three

Mrs. Byron stood at the serving table, pausing a moment to catch her breath after the mad flurry of food preparation. "Why don't you just hand me your plate, Sam," she said. "I hope you like paella. I know serving it from the pan like this isn't very formal, but it's the only way I know to keep it hot." She ladled onto the plate a large mound of seasoned rice dotted with chicken, shrimp, sausage, clams and peas. "Pip, would you move the candelabra? We aren't going to be able to see each other with them in the way. Put them over there. No, not there. That's too close to the flowers. Yes, there. Pour the wine, will you, darling?"

Sam watched as Pip's father tilted the bottle and poured white wine into her glass. She had grown accustomed to Mrs. Byron's slightly accented English.

What she never grew used to was the Spanish habit of serving wine with meals. In telling her parents about meals at Pip's house, Sam never mentioned the wine. She knew they would have found it hard to grasp that at the Byron's house wine was as normal as iced tea and, taken with a three-course meal, hardly more intoxicating.

After serving everyone, Mrs. Byron sat down. "I couldn't get fresh clams," she warned them. "These have been frozen."

"Tony Roscelli is flying down some lobsters from Maine for a church sale," said Mr. Byron. "I'm going to ask him if he can bring in some live clams for us."

"That would be lovely. Tell me the truth, all of you, can you tell I used canned broth instead of fresh stock? I did cook a bag of herbs in with it beforehand. That's supposed to take the canned flavor out."

"I like the canned flavor," said Pip.

"I didn't get any white meat," complained Terry. Pip's younger sister was at an age when she was all bones and knobby corners. From the looks of her she might have lived on celery sticks, but actually even at twelve she shared the Byron passion for food. Her dark hair was pulled back in a metal hair clasp that had no pretense at glamour, but she had Pip's tawny skin, his beautiful brown eyes and his serious expression. Maybe that was why Sam always warmed to Terry.

"Elbows off the table, please, Terry," said Mr. Byron.

"Why? Why do we have to keep our elbows off the table? Give me one good reason."

"So people will know we raised you right," said Mr. Byron. "That's why. End of subject."

"I think next time I'll put in more saffron. The rice doesn't seem to have enough character."

Sam recognized this as a typical conversation at the Byron's house. Whatever the Byrons happened to be talking about, whether it was flower arrangements or national defense, they were always working on improving it. At the very least they would be intent on keeping it up to the mark. They were perpetually evaluating things. It was like a nervous tic with them.

Sam wondered why she had even had the insane hope that Pip might go to Carolina instead of Yale. It wasn't just the Byrons' restless, questing quality that seemed to point their son toward out-of-state schools, it was also their slight foreignness, symbolized for Sam by the wine in her glass. Although the Byrons lived in Fenterville, they were not really rooted in North Carolina the way she was. They probably knew people from faraway places who said *ciao*, and *c'est la guerre*, people who played polo, people to whom diamonds as big as the one on Mrs. Byron's finger were the merest commonplace. For the Byrons, Pip's going away to school must have seemed only natural.

"There was something about Pip in the paper yesterday," Terry said, provocatively resting one elbow on the table.

"I didn't see it, and I always read the paper. You mean the local paper, don't you?" Mrs. Byron failed to notice the elbow.

"You're making it up," said Pip. "I wasn't in the paper. Why would I be in the paper?"

"You were, too! The kids were even talking about it at school."

"What are you telling us, Terry?" said Pip's father.

"Well, it didn't exactly mention him by name, but that's who it was about, all right. It was in the letters to the editor, that's why you didn't see it, Mom. There was this letter complaining about Pip's grades."

Pip got up from the table. "Let's just find out what this is all about, okay? Nobody's thrown out yesterday's paper, have they?"

A moment later Pip returned, folding the newspaper back to the inside front page. "Protest of zoning change, complaint about unleashed dogs—wait a minute, here it is. Who in the name of heaven is Hilda Starkey?"

"Give me that," said Pip's father.

"What does it say?" asked Sam.

Pip was frowning. "It's funny. It's about how transfer grades are calculated in figuring grade point averages. Terry, what makes you think it's about me?"

"Tommy Leonard's mom works in the office at the high school and she knows all about it."

Sam surveyed the table anxiously. The only Hilda she knew was Marcy's Aunt Hilda.

Pip's father frowned at the paper. "It seems this person is concerned with the weighting of the courses."

A look of comprehension dawned on Mrs. Byron's face. "It's about the letter St. Bartolf's sent, isn't it? How did they know about that?"

"Everyone knows everything in this town," said Pip's father irritably. "There's no such thing as privacy. Even so, I wonder if there hasn't been some breach of confidentiality. Somebody must have been dipping into Pip's records."

Sam was looking from one face to another, bewildered.

"You mean to say I'm the only person to transfer into this school? Nobody mentions me by name. What makes you think she's talking about me?"

"You're the only transfer student with a high grade point average," said Terry. "That's why. See, it comes down to who's going to be salutatorian. That's probably why this Hilda person is so bent out of shape. Obviously, if you were at the bottom of the class, it wouldn't matter what your average was, right? Besides, Tommy's mother knows everything. He's got the inside scoop. It's about you, all right."

"Who is this Hilda Starkey? I don't know any Hilda Starkey."

"Is somebody going to explain what's going on?" asked Sam desperately.

"It's this way," said Pip. "You know how they give extra weight to the honors courses?"

"Sure. Like with physics. An A counts more than an A in general science because physics is weighted. I follow you."

"Well, at Lee High you've got both general science and physics, say, but at St. Bartolf's they only had physics. They didn't have enough kids to offer both. It was the same way with English. Here you've got Advanced Placement English, which is weighted, and regular senior English, which isn't."

"St. Bartolf's just had Advanced Placement English?"

"I'm not sure whether they had Advanced Placement English. I transferred out before I got that far. But their English courses were very strong."

"It was a good school," Pip's mother put in.

"So anyway, when I transferred over here, St. Bartolf's wrote this letter saying that all their courses were honors courses and should be weighted."

"I thought you said they weren't big enough to have separate honors courses."

"They were a very strong school," said Mrs. Byron. "It amounted to the same thing."

"Besides," said Terry, "if they had had honors courses, you know Pip would have been in them. He's always been at the top of his class."

"I see what you're saying. So this Mrs. Starkey doesn't agree with the way the average was computed, right? She doesn't think those courses from St. Bartolf's should have been weighted."

"She doesn't come right out and say that. What she actually says is that the school board ought to establish a firm policy on how transfer credits are to be averaged," said Pip's father. He was still staring at the paper. "And that no exceptions should be made."

"They don't have a policy?"

"I suppose they usually just transfer them straight," said Pip. "But we had St. Bartolf's write a letter to the school for me. It didn't seem fair that my average would be dragged down just because I went to a small school my sophomore year. The level I had been at was the same as the honors courses here, so the letter was sort of a way to overcome a technicality, and the people at the school went along with it. It seemed fair to them, too."

"I'm surprised you were even thinking about that back when you were a sophomore."

"I transferred in at the beginning of my junior year, Sam. Sure, I was thinking about it. That's the year you sign up for the SATs and start picking out colleges. Naturally I knew that the first thing a college looks at is your class standing."

"It's a good thing you got out of St. Bartolf's, then," said Terry, licking her spoon. "First in a class of thirty doesn't look half as good as second in a class of five hundred."

"Terry, do not lick your spoon," said Pip's mother sharply.

"Pip, who's just behind you in the class standing?" asked his father.

"Lutisha Davis, last time I looked."

Sam was surprised he knew that. She couldn't have named the people whose grades were comparable to hers to save her life. But then Lutisha was the other Morehead nominee so maybe Pip just assumed that she was directly behind him in the class standing.

"You think Lutisha had something to do with this, Dad?"

"Well, *cuo bono*. Who benefits? Obviously, if your average were knocked down, this Lutisha Davis person might be salutatorian."

Pip frowned. "No, I don't think so. She really blew chemistry last year. She's a fair amount behind me. It's basically me and Marcy, neck and neck right up to the hundredth's decimal place or something, and then Lutisha's trailing a good many points behind. Even if my St. Bartolf's grades weren't weighted, I'd still be ahead of Lutisha. I can't see her behind this."

Sam couldn't see it, either. Lutisha was a sweet, quiet girl whose chief interest was the violin. She planned to go to a music conservatory. What did she care what Pip's grade point average was?

"Sam, has Marcy said anything to you about the grade averaging?"

"No. She was surprised you were right behind her in the class standing, that's all." Sam tried to make her face a blank. She had a growing conviction that Marcy had devised a way to check into Pip's records and that she had delegated her Aunt Hilda to make this howl of protest to the newspaper, but Sam hoped Pip's family wasn't going to ask her any more questions about it. That Pip and Marcy didn't get along had been awkward for her in a lot of little ways, but it had never been more awkward than this.

"How can people be so petty as to attack Pip in this underhanded way?" said Mrs. Byron, her voice quavering.

"You'd prefer they attack him by name, Isobel?"

"Who was talking about this at school?" Pip asked his sister. "I can't believe anybody would be interested."

"You'd believe it if you'd grown up around here the way I did," said his father. "The town is full of people who have nothing to do but gossip, and let's face it, the Byron family is their favorite target."

"Studies show that letters to the editor are the most frequently read feature," said Terry brightly.

"Oh, shut up, Terry."

"Don't speak that way to your sister, Pip. Theresa, dear, I wish you would try to learn a little tact and consideration for the feelings of others."

"Zowie," said Terry. "My brother is notorious!"

"That will be all, Theresa," said her father. "The letter is annoying, but I think the best thing we can do is ignore it."

"Let's not bring newspapers to the dinner table anymore, Phillip. It completely spoils my digestion. And I must say none of this is very amusing for Samantha. Would anyone care for more paella?"

The conversation for the rest of the meal was determinedly general, but Sam had the feeling that the letter to the editor was not very far from anyone's mind.

Sam didn't know what she thought about the weighting of the grades from St. Bartolf's. She could see how it would have looked to Marcy—a case of money, influence and special pleading. On the other hand, she could see Pip's point of view, too. He was one of the most able students in his class. Why should that truth be obscured by some technicality having to do with the averaging of the grades?

Pip drove her home after dinner. It was a cold night and Sam was grateful for the Mercedes's efficient heater.

"I'm never going to feel like I belong around here," Pip said. "People are always going to think of me as an outsider. They'll still be talking about how I transferred in here as a junior if I live in Fenterville a hundred years."

"You aren't thinking of making the experiment are you?"

"Live in Fenterville forever? Nah, not bloody likely. But that's not the point, Sam. I'm just trying to tell you there's this suspicion of outsiders around here. That's probably what that letter is all about."

"You're not an outsider. The Byrons are from around here. Your grandfather was Fenterville's leading citizen."

"You can stop right there. I don't want to think people accept me on the strength of my connection with that old bandit. Besides, it's not true. They don't accept me. They treat me like some foreigner. Look at Happy Chambers. Nobody likes her, but just because she went all the way through school with all the rest of you, she's part of the scenery. She fits in. I'm an interloper."

"You're upset about that letter," said Sam.

"Okay, maybe I am."

"I think you should listen to your father. A week from now nobody will remember it."

"It's not too much fun to realize somebody has got it in for you. This Hilda Starkey is just a front for someone, you know. Probably Marcy. Or could be Marcy's mother, if she's one of those pushy types. What do you think?"

"I don't know. But what does it matter? People are always writing letters to the editor, but it never comes to anything. It's just a way of blowing off steam."

"It gives me a queasy feeling, though. I can't help it."

"I wonder sometimes," Sam said hesitantly, "if it might have been better—for you, I mean—if we hadn't started going together practically as soon as you got here." She looked at him a little anxiously. "Maybe you would have gotten to know more people then, and then you wouldn't feel so much like an outsider."

"What an idea, Sam. You're the best thing that's happened to me here." He took one hand off the steering wheel and reached over to hold her hand. "You're my best friend. I'd be lost without you. Now you really are making me feel sick."

"You probably ate too much paella."

"No way, I was just picking at my food. I keep trying to remember whether I felt like I fit in back when we lived in Alexandria. Maybe the problem is me. I feel as if all my life I've been standing a little apart, watching. Watching myself, even. I wish I were one of those crazy guys that burbles insanely on about going to Hawaii and getting bombed on margaritas."

"I think it's in Mexico that they drink margaritas," said Sam.

"There you are. I can't get that right, either. I wouldn't even know how to begin getting bombed on margaritas, and if I did I'd just feel stupid doing it. I don't even see the point." He contemplated the road ahead with an expression of fixed gloom. "I never know what the scores are on the State and Carolina games."

"Well, that's a strike against your character."

"Believe me, it doesn't help. And I never can remember the punch lines to dirty jokes."

"Come on, you can't live your life wishing you were like somebody in a beer commercial. It's stupid. Look at it this way—you were elected Most Likely to Succeed. That doesn't sound like you're an outsider, does it?"

"I'm in the In Crowd, huh?"

"Obviously, people know who you are. They voted for you, didn't they?"

"They know the Byron name."

"You just won't let go of this, will you? And it's silly. Don't you know that most people like you? They do."

"Not Luke and Marcy."

"They're kind of a special case. The three of us used to be so tight, and I think Luke and Marcy have maybe never left off being a little bit resentful that I don't see so much of them since you came along. That's what my mother thinks, anyway."

"Sharp lady, your mother. You want to know what my mother thinks? She says because I'm a private sort of person, I'm always going to feel a little bit left out. She feels out of it, too."

"But she's living in a foreign country! She's got some excuse."

"And I'm just being neurotic. Is that what you're saying?"

"No, you're just being upset by that letter."

"I guess you never feel out of it, do you, Sam?"

"Well, I did grow up around here."

Pip looked at her in surprise, and Sam realized too late that she had undercut her own argument. Both of them laughed.

"Okay, I'm right, then," he said.

"Never. You're wrong."

"But you secretly think I'm right, don't you? You just admitted it."

"I don't know, Pip. You don't seem like an outsider to me. For me you're right at the center of things."

"I see what you mean. You aren't exactly an impartial observer." He returned his eyes to the road. "We'll have to ask Marcy for her opinion."

"So I got my Aunt Hilda to write that letter to the editor," Marcy said with satisfaction. "It's about time she was good for something."

"Don't tell me, Marce. I don't want to know."

"It's no secret. I'm not ashamed of it."

"But you must have gone into Pip's records! How could you do that?"

"Mrs. Smithers was sympathetic. That's how. She dug up Pip's file for me."

"No, I don't mean *how* could you do it, I mean, how could you *do* it? How would you like for somebody to go into your private records?"

"It would be okay with me. My life is an open book. I don't have anything to hide, unlike Pip."

"Those records are supposed to be confidential."

"Sam, my whole life is at stake here. This is no game. My grades are my only ticket out of here. They are literally my only asset. I have to sell them to the highest bidder to get to college. Don't you think I'm going to be upset when the integrity of the grading system is undermined? I had a feeling something was fishy when suddenly Pip appeared right beside me in the Morehead photo, out of the blue like that. I knew something had to be wrong, and I played my hunch."

Sam could feel a kind of fatal calm settling over her. She had tried to keep Marcy from telling her about the letter to the editor, but it had been useless. It couldn't be plainer that this was a case where she was going to be caught in the middle between Pip and Marcy, and she knew it would probably be smartest not to say anything at all. Still she felt she had to straighten Marcy out on one thing.

"Marce, think about it. Pip has made practically straight A's his entire high-school career. Do you think he did that by fiddling with the system? He's good at schoolwork, that's all. He made a practically perfect score on the SATs. It's cream to him. It's cream cakes and gumdrops."

Marcy was white around the mouth. "I don't want to hear it, Sam. The very last thing I want to hear, believe me, is how easy everything is for Pip. I am not in the mood."

"All I'm saying is that he belongs at the top of the class. There's nothing fishy about that. The only reason you didn't know that is because, well, he came in late, for one thing."

"That's what I'm saying, and it's the handling of those grades—"

"Let me finish, okay? He came in late, and also he doesn't like people talking about how smart he is. That's just the way he is. That's why it was a surprise to you."

"Look, Sam. Forget the surprise. Forget how I feel about having Pip be salutatorian. You know all about the letter that private school wrote to the administration. Can you honestly tell me you think that was fair?"

Sam hesitated. "I honestly can see there are two ways of looking at it, Marce."

Marcy threw up her hands. "I give up."

"Good. Because you know I can't choose between you and Pip, Marce. I love you both. Let's just let it be."

"The problem is that letter to the editor isn't going to get me anywhere," grumbled Marcy. "My mother even went over to the school and talked to Mr. Hendley. 'The grades are already computed. It's an administrative decision,' he said. 'If you think a change in policy is in order, take it up with the school board, and maybe something can be done about it with the next class.' The mealymouthed hypocrite."

After Marcy went home, Sam dragged herself downstairs, feeling suddenly tired. She understood Marcy's anger. She understood Pip's hurt. And she didn't see that there was any advantage to all that insight. She felt awful.

Her father was in the kitchen eating leftovers, and Sam told him the whole story while she fixed herself some tea. "Messy," was his comment.

"Marcy and Pip are a little bit nuts, don't you think? I mean, something is wrong when people are this caught up in grades. I used to think it was just Marcy, Dad, but now I can see that even if Pip doesn't say much about it, it's just as important to him. What difference does it make who's salutatorian? Who cares? Is it worth making yourself crazy over for years on end?"

"Look at it this way, Sam. Marcy and Pip have put in a lot of hard work making those grades. They need to think it was worth it." He sighed as he rose to rinse out his plate. "When I was a young idealistic teacher I used to think we ought to do away with grades entirely."

"I didn't know that. How come you've never talked about it?"

He shrugged. "I guess it started seeming to me that grades are a necessary evil. None of the alternatives anybody has tried have worked out any better. It's like money. You don't like the way it drives people crazy but you can't quite figure out how to get along without it. Sometimes I've seen my best and my brightest students actually get distracted by the grades. Rather than dig in to something that really interests them, they ration their time according to the payoff they can expect on the grade scale. It is sad, in a way. I'm glad you've never been one of those one-track minds."

"No danger! Anyway, I'll be glad when this blows over. I don't want to hear another word about grade point averages. Ever."

Chapter Four

Cold rain dripped from the leaden sky. It sifted through the pine trees in the Morrisons' front yard and fell quietly on the piles of heaped pine needles. On the front porch, Sam lifted the lid of the mailbox and felt a fluttering in her stomach as she saw the return address on the legal size envelope inside. She tore it open and let her breath escape in a sigh of relief. She had been accepted at Carolina after all.

Sinking onto the porch swing, she tried to conjure up a dimly remembered image from the time she had visited the campus when she was thirteen. A group of young women had been sitting in the brick pit outside of Carolina's student union, drinking colas out of paper cups. She recalled that the one wearing a halter had freckles on her back, and that the women's slap-dash clothes had seemed to her the height of sophistication. Books were heaped in careless stacks beside them, and all the sunny world seemed spread at their feet. Next year she would be one of them.

"Sam?"

She looked up, startled, to see Luke's mother climbing the steps to the porch, rain dripping from the hood of her raincoat. She was blond like Luke, with hair that matched her buff-colored raincoat, but her face had the puffy softness of a sedentary middle age. She normally had a brisk, commanding air about her, but this afternoon her shoulders were stooped, and she looked defeated, as if she had been crying. Sam realized with a twinge of sadness that Mrs. Lancaster was getting older. All of their parents were getting older.

"I hoped I would catch you at home," Mrs. Lancaster said. She sat down heavily. Her gaze rested on the torn envelope lying next to Sam on the swing. "The acceptances are starting to come in now, I see."

"Yes, I just got mine from Carolina. It's hard for me to believe that next year I'll be a college woman. I feel like I've barely gotten used to being a senior. Everything is going to be so different—being away from home, doing my own laundry." Sam realized she was talking quickly and nervously, as if to deflect Mrs. Lancaster from speaking, and she stopped abruptly.

"I thought you could tell me what's going on with Luke, Sam. Some people have started getting their college acceptances now, and he doesn't even seem to care. I thought when he realized that his friends were going off that he would have second thoughts. There are still places he could get in. Not competitive schools, but places where he could get a decent education."

"I don't think he wants to go to college."

"I can't accept that. I don't believe it."

Sam was silent.

"He's got a fine mind. He could do anything he wanted to. I refuse to believe that any son of mine wants to spend his life filling out classified ad forms. The waste! He is too young to make such an irrevocable and damaging decision."

"He never has liked schoolwork."

"But college is not like high school! That's what I've tried to make him understand. College is exciting! The rush of stimulating new ideas! Challenges! I know he'd love it if he'd give it a chance. 'Go just for one semester,' I told him. 'Then make your decision and I won't say another word. But to cut off your opportunity this way, to close yourself in from all sorts of possibilities when you're only eighteen, it doesn't make sense!' What has he said to you about this?"

Mrs. Lancaster stared at her intently, and Sam at once understood why there were never any discipline problems in Mrs. L.'s classroom. She gulped. "Just that he's made up his mind."

"Made up his mind!" Mrs. Lancaster made a helpless gesture. "He doesn't know what he's doing. He doesn't understand the significance of this decision. I've devoted myself to opening his eyes to the riches of ideas, the beauty of the arts, the joy of service to the community. This business of skipping college must be some sort of adolescent rebellion. I don't understand it."

Sam marveled that any parent could be so ignorant of her own child. If Luke's distaste for academics was adolescent rebellion then he had suffered from the longest adolescence in history.

"I don't think he hears anything I say anymore, Sam. I was hoping you might talk to him."

"It wouldn't do any good." Sam felt sorry for Mrs. Lancaster, because she had never had a chance in this fight. Not only was Luke fully as determined as his mother, but he was younger and stronger, and it was his life. "Maybe he'll decide to go to college later on."

"Society only allows us so long for an education. It can be hard to take up the threads once you have the responsibility for a family. He should know that after seeing the struggle Sarah McNair is having." The anxious look in Mrs. Lancaster's eyes made Sam suddenly realize why this pitch was not being made to Marcy. Luke's mother must be afraid that he was thinking of getting married. Maybe that was the only reason she could really believe in as a excuse for skipping college. She couldn't take it in that Luke simply disliked studying and was anxious to get to work. As if she suspected Sam of reading her mind, Mrs. Lancaster's eyes shifted. "I thought he might listen to you."

"He wouldn't. Besides, how can we even be sure what's right for Luke? It is his life."

"I certainly know my own son, Sam. And I think I've had enough experience of the world to know when he's making a dreadful mistake."

Sam maintained a polite silence.

"Promise me that you'll do your best to encourage him to give this some more consideration. Maybe when he sees how excited you are about going to college, it may have some impact on him. I'm always hearing about how important peer pressure is. Maybe it can be made to work for us in this case."

Sam knew Mrs. Lancaster was refusing to acknowledge some significant facts about Luke. Not only did he dislike schoolwork, but he burned with a passion for newspapers. Printer's ink was in his veins. Ever since he had gotten thrown off the school newspaper, he had been aching to get back in a newsroom, even if in a humble capacity.

Mrs. Lancaster rose. "Just promise me you'll do what you can, Sam."

They left it at that. Privately Sam knew that what she could do was exactly nothing.

Later that afternoon Sam heard a horn blow out front. When she appeared at the front door, Luke leaned out the window of his old green car. "Want to go for burgers?" he yelled. "We're celebrating. Marcy's gotten accepted everywhere."

"Hang on," called Sam. She ran inside to tell her father where she was going and to get her slicker.

Minutes later she squeezed in the front seat. Marcy fanned four envelopes out in her hand. "A full house!" she exulted. "They all want me!"

"That's great, Marce!"

"I've still got a couple I haven't heard from, but all these came in today's mail. Do you think it's computerized nationwide or something? This is amazing!"

"You deserve it."

"Now all I have to worry about is the money." The windshield wipers clacked monotonously.

"We'll worry about the money tomorrow," said Luke. "Today let's celebrate."

"It makes me feel *loved*!" Marcy cried ecstatically.

"Hey, these are just colleges we're talking about," said Luke. "Pull yourself together, kid."

"It makes me feel appreciated, anyway. All these years of slaving have finally paid off. They all offered me some kind of aid, Sam, but it's all in different packages and it's pretty complicated—different mixtures of grant and loan. All in all, I'd really be better off with the pricier schools since they seemed to offer more grant and less loan." She fished out one of the envelopes and held it out to Sam. "Stanford," she breathed reverently.

"All *right*!" said Sam. But she noticed that Luke's lips were tightening into a grim line, and she felt a pang of sympathy for him. You could hardly get farther away than Stanford. "I wonder if Pip has heard from Yale," she said uneasily.

"Not everybody has heard, not by a long shot. This is just what Mrs. Proctor calls the first or second wave of acceptances. They'll keep trickling in right on into spring."

"You must have been at the top of everybody's list to hear so soon."

"I know," sighed Marcy. "I'm really happy. And Stanford! My dream! The only problem is that even with the grants and the loans they offered me, I'm still over two thousand short, and that doesn't count books and the airfare out there. Two thousand plus is an awful lot of money."

"You can probably earn some of it working in the summer."

"Yes, it's a good thing I've worked right through high school and have some contacts. I'm pretty sure I'll be able to find something, even if those lawyers I'm working for don't need me in the summer. And most of the rest of the money I'll be able to make up with the Rotary Club scholarship. That one routinely goes to the valedictorian. Stanford, here I come! You can't imagine what this means to me, Sam. I'm not going to be Sarah McNair's pitiful little girl anymore. I'm going to be a student at one of the top schools in the country, and I did it all by myself! I did it!"

Luke put his hand out the window and banged on the outside of the car as he struck up a chorus of "Hail, Hail, the Gang's All Here." Marcy and Sam joined in. It was their old theme song, and Sam knew Luke had been prompted to begin it, probably for the same reason she was planning to take her teddy bear to college.

When they got to Wendy's, Sam made a stab at honoring her promise to Luke's mother. "Are you still planning to go to work for the *Banner*, Luke?"

"Sure. I've practically got it lined up. One of their girls is leaving in June to have a baby, and they're saying I can have her job slot."

"I just wonder if you might not be better off to go to college for a while first."

Luke stared at her incredulously. "Are you out of your mind, Sam? You know how what I think about that. We've been all over it."

Sam devoted herself to centering the pickle on her hamburger.

"Hey, wait a minute. Has my mother been leaning on you?"

Sam could feel her face growing warm. She cursed the moment she had ever agreed to say anything to Luke.

"Jeez, the nerve! Going behind my back to work on my friends! She couldn't get to me, so I guess she thought she'd come over and bully you."

"She's upset, that's all."

"She's crazy. Whose life is this, anyway? I can't believe she did that! Going around my back to my friends. She must think I'm some kind of mental defective. You're supposed to talk me around, huh? It's an insult, that's what it is. You'd think I was some idiot who went around with his mouth half open, waiting for some kind person to lead him by the hand. Or maybe she's hoping to cut me off from my friends, maybe that's it. She works on you and figures pretty soon I'll be fighting with you just the way I'm fighting with her. What a slimy mind she's got!"

"Don't tell her I told you!"

"Look, Sam, you don't have to be afraid of her. I'm not. You know, sometimes I look at my parents and I swear I have this sensation that we aren't even related. They could be somebody I met in the bus station. I don't have any respect for them. I just happen to live there. It's like being in a boarding house."

Sam was having a hard time swallowing her hamburger. She had never seen Luke so angry.

"She didn't say anything to you, Marcy, did she?" asked Luke.

Marcy shook her head. "She knows whose side I'm on."

"I just felt sorry for her," Sam protested. "I promised her I'd say something to you just to cheer her up some. She looked awful, Luke. She looked old."

"She wants her own way, that's all. She'd like to run my life the way she runs Dad's life. She's power mad, that woman. She'd do anything to get her way. No scruples at all. I can't believe she actually came over to work on you."

"She picked on you, Sam, because she knows you can always see everybody's point of view. That's what you get for being a softy," said Marcy.

Sam threw her hands up. "Okay, I felt sorry for her. So, sue me!"

"Cut it out, Sam. I didn't mean to yell at you. I know it's not your fault. I guess I'm freaking out. At home the pressure never lets up. It's like Chinese water torture; drip drip drip, and the next thing you know you're screaming. I just wonder when she's going to give up, that's all."

Sam picked up a french fry. "Some colleges still take people right into the summer."

"Trying to cheer me up, Sam? You forgot the drop-and-add period. You forgot about going in on the second semester. You know what she said to me Sunday? 'You're my son,' she said. 'I'll never give up on you.' I'm supposed to be grateful? She wants me to do exactly what she wants me to do, and I'm supposed to think she's some great kind of mother? I've got to figure out some way to get out of that house, that's all. I can go to work at the paper in June, and I figure if I moonlight at a convenience store and put in Saturdays at the lumber yard I might be able to split the cost of an apartment with Tommy Ledbetter."

"He does drugs," Sam warned.

"Hey, nobody's perfect."

Sam saw that the smile had left Marcy's face. Marcy was right, she thought. This idea that the senior year was easy was a myth. Between worrying about what was going to happen with your own life and worrying about what was going to happen to your friends, senior year was the hardest of all. In fact, there were ways in which it was remarkably like taking a running jump off a cliff.

Getting out of his car in the rain, Pip saw Sam and her friends at a table in the brightly lit interior of Wendy's. It gave him a perverse satisfaction to see that none of them looked happy. When he had called at Sam's house and discovered she was out, he had been haunted with fantasies that she was having a gay old time with Luke and Marcy, leaving him to drive around in the rain alone. Inside Wendy's the normally cool Luke was gesturing like Trotsky in some filmstrip. Pip could see that Marcy's head was bent over her milk shake as if she were avoiding looking at Luke, and Sam sat stiffly in a posture Pip recognized as anxious. This was no happy little party.

He hesitated a second when he reached the door, but then swiftly opened it and walked in. Sam, feeling the gust of wind, turned around, and seeing him, grinned and waved both her arms. Her delight at seeing him set Pip's blood humming with pleasure. He only wished he could make the other two kids disappear.

When he brought his order to the table, for once he had the peculiar sensation that Marcy and Luke were actually relieved to see him. He pulled up a chair and began to unwrap his burger, shooting an inquiring glance at Sam.

"Marcy's gotten accepted at Stanford," Sam explained, "and also to practically everyplace else. This is a kind of celebration." He heard the doubtful note in her voice.

"Congratulations," Pip said. He lifted his eyes from his burger to look at Marcy. He hadn't forgotten for a minute about the letter to the editor. Luckily, he knew he did not have the sort of face that gave away what he was thinking. "I heard from a couple of places myself today," he said, "but not my first choice, yet."

"Oh, and I got accepted at Carolina!" Sam added.

Pip smiled and gave her knee a squeeze under the table. It was typical of Sam that she would forget her own news in the rush of telling other people's.

There was a long silence, and Pip looked at the others. "The thing is," Sam said, "all this happiness has kind of bowled us over. That's how it is."

Luke threw his napkin on the table and laughed. "I've been spouting off about my parents, Byron. That's why everybody's looking shell-shocked. Want to buy a pair of parents, real cheap?"

"No, thanks, I've got parents enough already."

"I would think yours would be tickled pink with you."

"Well, they do sort of worship the ground I walk on. Is that the kind of thing you mean?"

"Yeah, I bet they do. You keep your nose clean, apply to Ivy League schools. Quite the good little boy, aren't you?"

Sam eyed Luke nervously. "Don't mind Luke, Pip. He doesn't know what he's saying."

"Wait a minute, I see what you're getting at," Pip said. "You're saying if I messed up my life good, let my grades slip and got into trouble with the law, I'd be more like one of the guys."

Luke flushed. "It's not my fault you had to bail us out that time," he said. "I didn't ask you to, and I didn't expect you to go throwing it up to me."

"Excuse me. In the future I'll do my best to measure up to your high standards."

Sam was waving a napkin between them. "Truce!" she said. "White flag. Come on, you guys."

"I'm sorry, Byron," Luke said stiffly. "I guess I'm kind of on edge."

"It's being seniors," Sam said. "We're all going a little crazy. Do you remember when we thought all there was to senior year was getting to sit around the senior fountain?"

"Days of innocence," said Marcy. "Do you know I've already started having nightmares about college? I dream that I've been taking French all semester but I forget to go to the classes and suddenly it's exam time. Or like last night, I dreamed I couldn't figure out my class schedule and couldn't find *any* of my classes and all the time I was getting more and more behind."

Sam said, "I hate to tell you this, Marce, but my dad told me he had that dream until he was thirty."

"Good grief, really? This is what I've got to look forward to?"

"And when he quit dreaming that, he started dreaming that he had shown up to teach his class and suddenly realized that he hadn't prepared it!"

They all laughed, but Pip was watching the others with curious eyes.

He gave Sam a ride home afterward. The rain had let up but the roads were slick. Water hissed under the wheels of the car, and the traffic lights reflected on dark mirrored surfaces.

"It's just as well you showed up when you did," Sam said. "I think Marcy and Luke want to be alone."

"We want to be alone, too, don't we? You don't have to get right home, do you?"

"I don't think we'd better go someplace and park, if that's what you mean. I'm still all churned up about that business with Luke."

"You need me to comfort you, that's what."

"I think you'd better take me home, Pip."

His hand brushed against her softly. "Okay," he said. "I'm sorry you're upset."

"Don't you see how everything is changing? *We're* changing. Ever since I got that acceptance from Carolina this afternoon, I've felt different. It's real. It's going to happen after all. We're going to college."

"This comes as a shock to you?"

"You don't understand. I have these flashes where it's almost as if I'm at college looking back on all this. It feels very strange. I'm going out with new boys, strangers, and I see myself laughing nervously and talking about movies and high school and Fenterville. Small talk, you know. 'Have you read any good books lately?' That kind of thing."

"I don't like the part about going out with other boys."

"I don't like it, either. After being so close to someone, all that will be like acting in a play. Not real."

Pip figured he had a solution to that—don't go out with all those strange boys. But he thought that to say that would seem churlish. Sam was looking out the window, and her profile was outlined by lights from the nearby shopping center.

"We'll work something out, Sam. Going away to college isn't the end of the world. Aren't you excited about it just a little bit?"

"I do remember being kind of excited before all that awful drama with Luke and his mother."

"Luke's mother is his problem."

"So you think I should concentrate on the excitement and new challenges ahead."

"Something like that."

Sam laughed but she didn't really sound amused. She's too sensitive for her own good, Pip thought. She worries too much about other people.

When Sam got home, her parents were reading in the living room.

"You didn't tell me you got accepted at Carolina!" her mother exclaimed. "I found the envelope on the kitchen table."

"Yup, I got accepted."

"That's wonderful. To get your first choice, and so early in the year. Now you're all set. None of that uncertainty and doubt. I'm surprised you didn't call me at work to tell me."

"I guess I'm getting blasé." Sam threw herself into the easy chair by the fireplace. "Actually, the truth is it slipped my mind. Luke's mother came over this afternoon and begged me to persuade Luke not to go to work at the newspaper.''

Her father laid his paper onto the hassock. ''What on earth does she think you can do?''

''I don't know. She just can't accept it that Luke won't go to college.''

''Greatest mistake in the world to go if you aren't interested,'' her father said promptly. ''Complete waste of money.''

''Come on, Larry. You know that if Sam or Robin had decided to skip college, you would have had a conniption.''

''No, I wouldn't. We could take a world cruise with the money we saved. But it's an academic question. No daughter of mine would be so stupid as to pass up the advantage of an education.''

''That's just the kind of thing Mrs. Lancaster was saying this afternoon, Dad. She can't believe Luke would skip college.''

''She ought to be used to disappointment by now. Luke hasn't done a thing he was supposed to since he was born. What on earth made her think he was going to suddenly click his heels and say 'yes, ma'am,' when he turned seventeen?''

Sam's mother reached for her mending basket. ''If you ask me, the problem in that family is Carl.''

''Carl? Why blame him, Ginny? He hasn't done a thing.''

''That's what I'm saying. He doesn't do anything. Carl is so passive that Luke never had a model of a male being properly assertive. So in his effort to assert himself against his mother, he's just ended up being wild.''

"You're sounding like a social worker again."

"Well, do you honestly think I'm wrong?"

"I don't know. Something's wrong, all right. Luke never has had any respect for authority, and I don't think it's an accident. Maybe it comes down to some problem with his parents."

"I think you're right," said Sam. "He doesn't respect them. That's what he was just telling me."

"It's ironic, really, when you think about it," said her father. "Probably no one on the faculty is more respected than Eloise, and she can't influence her own son."

"I think she feels it very much, Dad."

"It's Carl," said her mother. "He never backs her up. I never could understand what she saw in him."

Sam had never heard her parents be so frankly critical of Luke's father. In a strange way it pleased her. She had the feeling they were beginning to think of her as an adult and that they no longer felt such a need to censor their thoughts for her childish consumption.

"Mrs. Lancaster's afraid Luke is going to get married," Sam said.

There was an awful silence.

"It's ridiculous, of course," she went on. "Luke is absolutely crazy about Marcy. If he were going to marry anybody he'd marry her, and Marcy has no intention of getting married. Nothing is going to stop her from going off to Stanford."

"What did Eloise actually say to you, Sam?"

"Well, she didn't come right out and *tell* me that's what she was worried about, if that's what you mean, but I could see the cold fear in her eyes when Marcy's name came up. It seemed pretty stupid to me. I can think of a lot better things to worry about. It's not as if getting married is so awful. Look how happy you two have been. Look at Gram and Grampa! What's so bad about loving somebody so much you want to spend the rest of your life with him?''

On that exit line Sam went upstairs to get her bath. She would have been surprised to see that her parents were looking at each other uneasily.

Chapter Five

Pip's acceptance from Yale came in March. His mother called his father's office to leave word of the happy news, and Pip at once called Sam.

"I got my acceptance from Yale."

"That's wonderful! I'm so happy for you, Pip."

He realized that he would have preferred for her response to be a sharp intake of the breath, even a cry of pain.

"Of course I'm very happy," he said.

"You don't sound very happy."

"You should see the tears of joy in my eyes."

"But isn't this just what you wanted?"

"'Take what you want,' said God, 'and pay for it.'"

"What?"

"Old Spanish proverb. When can I see you?"

"Now, I guess. I'm washing the car, but—"

"I'm coming right over."

When he opened Sam's front door she was coming down the stairs buttoning up her shirt. Her hair was wet and scored with comb marks, and her cutoff jeans looked faintly damp, too.

"I showered as fast as I could," she said.

He looked at her appreciatively. "You don't have to get dressed on my account."

Sam shot an apprehensive look toward the kitchen.

"Let's go somewhere," said Pip. "Anywhere."

"Okay, I'll tell Mom. When do you think we'll get back."

"Never. Late. Tomorrow. Sometime."

"I'll say we're going for a drive and we're not sure when we'll be back."

"Cassandra's packed us a hamper. I thought we could have a picnic."

As they drove away from the house, Pip stole a glance at Sam and thought about sex. Even if you came up with a substitute for the procreation part, and even if you didn't care about the fun, he thought, you might still crave the closeness. He couldn't think when he had wanted so much to press Sam close to him. He was lonely in a way he had never been before. It was as if he were already tasting the loneliness of next year.

Sam flashed him an understanding look. "Don't worry. Everybody has a weird feeling when they get the acceptance they've waited for. Marcy freaked out, I freaked out, now it's your turn. It doesn't mean anything. In a little while you'll start feeling more normal. I'll bet your dad was really excited about your getting in. What did he say?"

"I haven't talked to him yet. He was over at his office having a strategy meeting."

"Oh, right. The campaign for governor."

"Yeah, they're toying with the slogan Phillip Byron—Friend to Education."

"Not a good idea. Hardly anybody is interested in education. It's better for him to have old war wounds and to be Friend of the Little People."

"Friend to midgets? I never knew they were much of a voting block."

"No, idiot. By little people I mean ordinary people who have to work for a living. He needs to wear a plaid shirt, or if he wears a white shirt he has to unbutton it, roll up the sleeves and throw his coat over one shoulder."

"You're making this up."

"Gospel, Pip, I swear. That's why women don't get elected to high office. It's because when they unbutton their shirts and sling their coats over their shoulders they look like slobs. Only men can get away with being a friend to the little people."

"I'll have to get Dad to hire you as a political adviser."

"A great idea—as it happens I don't have a summer job lined up yet."

When they got to the park Pip spread out plastic sheeting over the wet ground, and Sam helped him arrange the quilt on top of it. A large dogwood nearby still dripped with the morning's rain. Perhaps because it was still so damp, the park was all but deserted. As they unpacked the picnic hamper, a jogger bobbed by, his head just visible over the tall bank of azaleas near them. Except for that, they might have been alone in the world. The only sound was the noise of ducks squabbling in the nearby pond.

Pip pulled out a corkscrew to open the bottle of wine. Sam darted a look around. "Be careful," she said. "If a cop sees us we could be raked in for drinking underage and having an open container in a park."

"All that for having a glass of wine with lunch? You know, there's something kind of uncivilized about Fenterville."

"What do you care? In a matter of months you'll be up at New Haven."

Gloomily, Pip popped the cork out of the bottle. He didn't see why she had to look so indecently pleased. "Nobody can see us over here, anyway. We're shielded from the road, and if I ever saw a cop on foot in this town I'd faint." He poured the wine into the plastic glasses.

"Maybe we ought to toast your new life at Yale."

"No," Pip said firmly, raising his glass. "To us."

"To us, then."

This was not going quite the way Pip had planned. On his list of scheduled events had been a passionate embrace on the quilt. Sam was over on the other side of the bread and goat cheese, and here he was by the picnic hamper. It seemed as if there was a vast expanse of quilt between them, and he couldn't quite figure out how to casually get over there to work up to the passionate embrace. He realized that the reason for that was that his nerves were totally shot. Grimly, he cut himself a piece of goat cheese and ate it. Great, he thought. Now his breath would smell of goat cheese. He should have mapped out a more precise game plan.

"You aren't mad at me or anything, are you?" asked Sam.

He groaned and leaned his head on his hands. "No, of course, I'm not mad at you. Getting this acceptance in the mail has just got me off balance. I was starting to worry that I wasn't going to get in after all, and then all of a sudden it came."

Sam edged over next to him and tentatively put her arm around him. "Nobody died."

Pip almost laughed out loud. He had been sitting there as much as paralyzed wondering how to get around to Sam's side of the quilt and then she had come to him. She was always anticipating what he needed and meeting him more than halfway. It wasn't as if she read his mind, exactly. It was more that she read his feelings. Suddenly confident, he put his arms around her and kissed her, pressing her down to the quilt.

"Sam, marry me," he said breathlessly.

Her eyes widened, and she gently pushed his hair out of his face.

"Well, yes or no?"

"Golly, have you talked to your parents about this?"

"Dammit, Sam, you don't talk to your parents about getting married. You just do it."

"Well, if you're underage you need their permission, and then there's the money angle, whether you expect them to still put you through college and everything."

He sat up. "You can stop it right there. I'm getting all choked up with the romance of the moment. For Pete's sake, do you want to marry me or not?"

Sam sat up and put her hands on his shoulders. "I'd love to marry you, Pip."

"Well, all right then. That's settled. You don't have to worry about the money. Grandfather left me a third of his stock in the company."

"He did? Why would he do a thing like that?"

Pip shrugged. "To beat the government out of inheritance taxes, I guess, and I wouldn't be surprised if he had some weird fantasy of me and Dad engaged in some internecine struggle for control. That was the kind of thing he loved. You know what a hostile old creep he was. Anyway, you'd be marrying a rich man, but I only get the income until I'm twenty-three."

"So you aren't joking about this."

"The Byrons never joke about money."

"I mean about the getting married part."

"Well, it doesn't strike me as hilarious, to tell you the truth. I don't know how it hits you."

"It strikes me as lovely and sweet," she said. She lifted his hand and kissed it. "But we can't get married now."

"Well, not now, but as soon as we graduate. You don't have to worry about my parents, Sam. They'll come around. You don't mind converting to Catholicism, do you?" He looked at her anxiously, then added quickly, "Not that you have to or anything. We can work something out. About the kids, I mean."

"I don't mean now as in March," she explained patiently, "I mean now as in this-time-in-our-lives."

"Hey, wait a minute. You just told me yes!"

"Well, I certainly didn't want to say no. I don't see how I could possibly love anyone more than I love you, but I can't get into Yale. What am I supposed to do while you're at school? Sit around the apartment and twiddle my ignorant thumbs?''

"There are other schools around there you could go to.''

"I'd still be sort of trailing after you, though. And what if you get up there and meet new people and wish you were free? No, it's just not right.''

"I guess you're looking forward to Carolina and all those parties," Pip said bitterly.

"There's nothing wrong with going to parties. That's what you're supposed to do when you're young. And you learn all kinds of things and try out things and meet lots of new people.'' Sam grinned at him. "And after four years or so you figure you haven't seen anybody you like better than Pip and then you go and marry him if he'll still have you.''

"Four years is a long time.''

"Life is a longer time. You don't want to be sitting around when you're thirty wondering what you missed out on.''

"I'm not so much worried about what I might miss as about who I might lose.''

"That's how you feel now. It might look pretty different to you a year from now when you're up there with all those sexy, intellectual Yankee girls.'' She shivered. "If I keep going I'm going to be talking myself into getting married.''

"Go right ahead.''

"Nah. It's not a good idea, and deep down you know it.''

"Want some spiced beef?" he asked, reaching for the knife. "Cassandra's spiced beef is famous. Though not perhaps as perfect as her chocolate cake, about which, more anon.''

"You do understand what I'm saying, don't you, Pip?"

"I guess so."

"And you're not mad at me, are you?"

"Good grief, Sam. No, I'm not mad at you."

Actually, Pip was feeling almost relieved. She hadn't said no, after all. She did love him. And if the truth were told, didn't he have enough to deal with right now just graduating and going away to school without getting married on top of it?

When Pip got home, his mother was bent over the dining room table with a pair of scissors.

"Whistling?" she said. "You must be happy."

"So-so." He shrugged. "What are you clipping out?" He peered over her shoulder at the newspaper. "'Byron Tobacco Company Presents Awards in Education.'"

"It's a good picture of your father, don't you think?"

"I guess. Hey, that's Mrs. Lancaster! You know, my English teacher, Luke's mother. She does all the Advanced Placement English." Pip skimmed the article and learned that the company was presenting three $1,000 awards, one each at the grammar-school, junior-high and high-school levels, to teachers outstanding in skill and leadership. He presumed this was part of the buildup for Phillip Byron—Friend of Education.

"Luke's mother, you say? I can't say I see the resemblance."

"She's old and ugly, and he's eighteen and gorgeous. What kind of resemblance do you expect? But it's Luke's mother, all right. She's a good teacher. I'm not surprised she got the award."

Pip went on upstairs to his room, still whistling.

When Luke got home that afternoon he saw the picture of the awards ceremony had been roughly torn out of the paper and pinned to the bulletin board in the kitchen. He already knew about the award, of course, since he had attended the presentation banquet with his parents. Glancing at the clipping with faint annoyance, he recalled that his mother had taken it for granted that he would attend the ceremony. He got no credit for anything he did these days. Her attention was focused solely on his supreme rebellion—his refusal to go to college.

The awards banquet had been about what he had expected—the food had been bad, the speeches worse, and he had had to listen to his mother burble all the way home about what a fine figure of a man Phillip Byron was. Luke hated ceremonies. He disliked the way they exaggerated the importance of the trivial events they celebrated, he disliked the way audiences sat still in their seats staring at the speakers like sheep, and he disliked the canned music, the canned patriotism and the canned speeches that tended to surface on ceremonial occasions.

Of course, the all-time horrible ceremony had been the senior-awards ceremony at school. He had not really expected to be given any award, and when Denny Parker's froggy voice had called out "Most Attractive—Luke Lancaster," his first response had been nausea. Luckily, he had been sitting by the fire door, and almost before anyone turned around to stare at him, he had been out of there, taking deep breaths in the clean air of the school yard. Nobody who knew him well had been really surprised when he had not shown up on stage, but he had had to put up with a lot of kindly sympathy from Delia Rosenthamer, who kept going on about her stage fright at piano recitals and how basically shy she was, until he had been forced to say something really rude to get rid of her.

It was too bad that all of his problems could not be so easily solved. He took the clipping down from the bulletin board and looked at it critically. It was a bad picture. All of the pictures in the *Banner* were bad because there was no staff photographer. The *Banner* was a small, low-budget operation, and reporters, after attending a one-day workshop on how to operate a camera, took their own pictures. Not that there was any disgrace in a newspaper's being small. Most of the newspapers in the country were low-budget operations, and it stood to reason that most reporters started out by working for just such papers. But Luke found himself envying Marcy. Ever since that acceptance had arrived from Stanford, she had walked as if buoyed up by some unseen flotation device. In contrast Luke felt earthbound and directionless. He could get a job doing classified ads on the *Banner*, all right, but it wasn't clear to him how to get from there to the kind of job he really wanted, news reporting.

What he needed was a nice war. He instinctively felt that there wouldn't be too much competition when it came to covering combat zones. And for covering a war you didn't need a degree from some prestigious journalism school. War was a place where cold nerve and the ability to think on your feet would pay off. Unfortunately, no suitable war seemed to be at hand. There was the mess in Lebanon, of course, but reporters were getting kidnapped over there. Luke had no objection to being blown up by a land mine, but he disliked the idea of being kidnapped by some freakos who would tie you up and give you nonstop political speeches. It would be, he thought, entirely too much like attending a ceremony.

Looking down he saw that he was holding a wad of newsprint. He stared for a moment in puzzlement before he realized that he had unconsciously crushed the newspaper clipping in his hand. He spent a second or two wondering how he could explain to his mother that this didn't indicate some deep-seated hostility to all she stood for. Then he shrugged. It was hopeless. He lit the gas jet on the stove and fed the wadded clipping to the flame. A moment later all that remained was a thin shred of ash. Luke thrust his hands in his pocket and strolled out of the kitchen. Let her figure it out.

When Sam got home from her picnic with Pip, her mother called to her from the kitchen. "Sam, guess what? Ty just sat up all by himself. Robin called a few minutes ago. Golly, they grow up fast! One day you bring them home from the hospital with their head lolling about and this gaga expression on their faces. The next thing you know they're pulling books off the shelves, asserting their personalities and the house is in an uproar. Then just when you've got used to the commotion, they're off to college!" Her mother wiped her eyes with the corner of her apron.

Sam did not really understand why her mother was getting all soupy and sentimental. It was not as if Sam's going away to college were some big surprise. At the moment, she herself was feeling quite calm about it. She glanced at the newspaper on the kitchen table. "Hey, it's Luke's mom. Did you see this picture in the paper?"

"Yes. Be careful and don't spill anything on it. I'm going to clip it out to give to Eloise. She may want extra copies."

"Gee, she won a thousand dollars! That's a lot of money."

"It's about time somebody took some notice of education. You get a lot of lip service, but this is the first time I can remember anybody shelling out actual cash in recognition of teaching skills."

"Maybe if they make it an annual event, Dad will win it one of these days."

"Maybe so. Personally, I would feel tempted to use it to re-cover the living-room chairs, but I think the idea is that you're supposed to spend the money on professional training or course materials. I expect Eloise will do just that. That's the way she is. Uptight and gung ho on education."

"It sure is an irony that she's Luke's mother."

Sam's mother began beating eggs with energy. "I don't know about that. How many kids do you know that are just like their parents? It's not unusual for kids to rebel against their parents' values. Not that it's happened to us, yet." She superstitiously knocked on the wood-grain Formica of the counter.

Sam opened the refrigerator and pulled out the milk and the rest of the cake.

"I thought you and Pip were going on a picnic," said her mother. "Are you hungry again already?"

"I guess I sort of forgot to eat."

Sam quickly polished off the milk and the cake and then went on upstairs, humming, unaware that her mother's eyes were following her anxiously.

When she got to her room, Sam pushed her hair up with both hands and looked at herself in the mirror. At last, she thought, it had happened. She had grown up. And despite what her mother had said, it did not seem to her that it had happened quickly at all. She remembered it had seemed like an eternity before her feet reached to the floor from the couch, and even longer until she was able to reach the top of the refrigerator where the donuts were kept. Slowest of all had been those years between eleven and the magic year of sixteen when she had achieved a driver's license. But none of these milestones had been as important to her as what she could feel, a warm and growing sense that she would be able to handle life on her own.

She wondered what her mother would think if she knew Pip had just proposed. She would probably pass out. Sam had to sit down on the bed and breathe deeply to keep from giggling because she was just slightly light-headed from excitement and from her heart pounding whenever she thought of Pip. When she thought of how controlled he was, how carefully and prudently he managed his life, she felt deeply touched that he had made such an impulsive and ill-considered offer. That he was serious about it, she didn't doubt for a minute. When Pip said something, he meant it.

He had caught her by surprise, but maybe in another way she had not been entirely surprised. They were so right for each other that anybody might think of getting married. She had thought of it herself. She had been mulling over the idea almost since she had met Pip. She wasn't sure how she had come to the conclusion getting married now would be a bad idea. It was not simply a matter of knowing that most teenage marriages don't last, of knowing that their parents would cut up rough and that all their friends would think it was a stupid thing to do. It was something deeper than that, something as deep as her heart. She felt she needed space and time. She wanted a chance to be one of those sun-touched girls she had seen at Carolina.

Chapter Six

I'm sorry, Sam. I'm going to have to rework the organization on that senior thesis, and that means all the footnotes have to be renumbered. I can't figure out why I didn't see it sooner. But there it is. Reworking it like that, it's going to take me all weekend to make sure the seams don't show."

Sam took a deep breath. "Right. Well, I think I'm going anyway. I'll tell you all about it."

After Pip hung up, Sam glanced at her own senior thesis, neatly bound in a folder on her desk, and was glad to be the sort of person who was content with a B. The grade of B was wide and forgiving. Anything clean, decently written and showing a reasonable amount of intelligence rated a B. It was only because Pip had his heart set on an A that he was going to have to miss the concert tonight. Teachers were notoriously picky and temperamental about dishing out A's.

The phone on the bedside table rang, and Sam reached for it.

"Sam? Have you seen Luke?"

"No, Marce. When would I have seen Luke? Up till last night I was, like everyone else, slaving away on my senior thesis. It's all finished now, though." Sam could not keep the smug note out of her voice.

"I thought I was finished, too, but now I see I left out a half a page." Marcy groaned. "The last third of it is going to have to be retyped. It would be suicide for me to go out tonight. I just can't take the chance, but I can't seem to get hold of Luke to tell him. We were going to that Black River Chorus production. I told him it was a mistake to get the tickets. I just knew something like this would happen. Besides, even if I didn't have to retype the last third of it, I should spend every minute I have making sure it is absolutely perfect. Maybe I'll see something else that needs work during my reading and rereading and rereading of it this weekend."

"Don't worry, Marce. Luke probably expected something like this. Pip just called me and canceled out, too."

"So he's spending all weekend on his, too, huh? That makes me feel just great. Believe me I can't afford to be out frivoling when people like Pip have got their nose firmly to the grindstone."

"Quit tearing your hair."

"How did you know I was tearing my hair?"

"Lucky guess. Look, Marce, go in peace. Embrace your footnotes. Take comfort in your bibliography. Find fulfillment in chasing the elusive A."

"You don't have to get nasty with me, Sam. I'm not the one who stood you up."

Marcy hung up abruptly.

Sam put on her tennis shoes and went outside. Her father was pruning a shrub in the front yard. "Where are you off to?" he asked.

"I'm off to enjoy the soft coming of summer," she said stiffly. "Alone."

Her father grinned. "Have a fight with Pip?"

"Not exactly. He just called to say he needs to spend all weekend on his senior thesis."

"Very wise."

"Very wise! What kind of a comment is that? Don't you think there's a limit to the amount of time people should spend on their schoolwork? Don't you think people should take time to live, for example? We were supposed to go to hear the Black River Chorus tonight."

"What do you expect me to say, Sam? I'm a teacher. I think like a teacher."

Sam got in her car and drove to Halstead Park. She parked beside the lake and watched a mother duck leading some adolescent ducklings in a long flotilla toward the island in the center. Behind her was the tall green bank of azaleas that had been covered with flowers only weeks ago.

She realized she was being silly and childish to be annoyed about Pip's canceling out on her at the last minute. She would get over it in a minute if she just leaned against her car, watched the V-shaped wake left by the ducks and considered the enormous size of the universe. Suddenly something stung her ear, and Sam wheeled around to see Luke holding a handful of acorns.

"Did you throw one of those acorns at me?"

"Pretty good aim, huh?" He sidestepped a bag of squashed fast food and came over to her.

"What are you doing here?"

"Getting out of the house. I'm trying to spend most of my time out since Mom started her latest last ditch effort to show me the value of a good education."

"Marcy's been trying to call you."

"I need a mobile unit, that's what. Why's she trying to call me? I'm going to be seeing her in—" he glanced at his watch "—less than an hour. We're taking a picnic to the Black River Chorus thing. They're doing it at Donner Farm this year."

"I know. Pip and I were going. Marcy called because she ran into trouble with her senior thesis and is canceling out. It's the same story with Pip."

Luke grimaced. "Oh, heck. I'm going to be up to my ears in sandwiches. I've already packed the stuff in the car."

"Have you got your thesis finished?"

"Well, I've got the notes and everything. I thought I'd write it up tomorrow. I have a pretty good idea what I'm going to say. It's just a matter of throwing it all together."

Sam thought of the vast gulf that yawned between Pip's approach to the senior thesis, which required scheduled hours at the library from September to June, and Luke's, which could be loosely summed up in the words "faking it."

"Let's you and me go to the chorus thing," Luke suggested. "You can help me eat all those sandwiches."

"Okay. You know, if we'd taken a better look at the calendar we'd have known Pip and Marcy were going to flake out on us. It was in the cards."

"I don't know. I was thinking Marcy would let up on the work a little bit. I mean, when we got up close to graduation. She knows she got into Stanford. What's she killing herself for?"

"She's got the valedictorian thing to worry about, I guess."

"Everybody knows Marcy's going to be valedictorian—it's not that, Sam. It's a habit, like cigarettes. She's been killing herself so long she doesn't know how to stop."

An hour later Luke and Sam sat on a blanket amid a crowd of other couples who had brought picnic dinners.

Sam bit into a peanut-butter-and-jelly sandwich, conscious of dampness seeping through the blanket. Now that the sun had set it really wasn't that warm anymore, and she wished she had brought a jacket.

A trio was playing on a platform erected in front of the rail fence. Out of the corner of her eye Sam could see members of the chorus, in evening dress, darting in and out of the barn, looking harassed.

"Yo!"

Reggie was making his way between the blankets to them. He was wearing a white suit with a white carnation.

"Hi, Reg. You're looking sharp."

"Yolanda's over by the barn but she didn't think she'd better try getting across all this grass in those high-heeled shoes of hers. Where are Pip and Marcy?"

"They're working," said Luke.

"Those two missed Homecoming, too, didn't they? That makes them certified workaholics, if you ask me. Stomp it out before it spreads. Hey, we miss you guys on the newspaper staff. It hasn't been the same since you went away."

"You sound like a memorial on the obit page." Luke reached for another sandwich. "That's what I'll probably be doing this time next year, Reg, working on the obituary page of the *Banner*. Which is fine. It's a little closer to the newsroom than I am now, anyway."

"Next year! Don't talk to me about next year," groaned Reggie. "I have to make up my mind about my college, and I mean quick. What do you think? Should I go to N.C. Central or East Carolina? I mean, this is keeping me up nights, no joke. See, if I go to N.C. Central I'm sure of having a really great social life, feeling real comfortable, no communication problems, you know what I mean?"

"Go with that, then," said Luke. "Sounds good. I go for comfort."

"I don't know though. Maybe I don't want to be in a ghetto-type situation. Maybe I ought to go to a white school. It might look good on my record, you know. Shows I can cut it with all that pressure. Shows I can mix."

"I'd do that," said Sam. "You get along with everybody, Reg. You don't have to worry about your social life. You need to be thinking about how it's going to look to somebody hiring you. What does Mrs. Proctor tell you?''

"She tells me East Carolina, but what does she know? She's not the one putting her life on the line. It's driving me crazy. One day I think I've made up my mind, I sleep on it, and the next morning I'm thinking something else again."

"Flip a coin," suggested Luke.

"Hey, man, this is my life we're talking about here. This is not a coin-flipping situation. This is serious."

Luke leaned back on his elbows. "Nothing is serious, Reg."

"I've got it!" said Sam. "Go to East Carolina and try it out, and if you hate it you can transfer to Central, right?"

"Except that would really show I couldn't cut it. It's not like if I just decide to go to Central in the first place, right? It's like—failure."

Luke picked up another sandwich. "You're going to give yourself a coronary if you keep this up."

"Don't I know it," said Reg gloomily. "Hey, I guess I better get on back to Yolanda or else she's going to be suing me for desertion. See you around."

They watched the white-suited figure making its way back toward the barn. "Will you get a load of that?" said Luke. "Ole Reggie's a nervous wreck. Reggie! I never thought I'd see it."

"If senior year were a car," said Sam, "it would be recalled."

Luke grinned. "If it were a rock star it would look like Alice Cooper."

"If it were a note, it would be flat."

"If it were a cat, it would be pregnant."

"If it were a boyfriend," said Sam, "it would be working on its senior thesis."

They heard discordant sounds and realized the orchestra was beginning to tune up.

"Shh," said Luke. "This is the part I like the best."

Sam hugged her knees and prepared to enjoy herself. She was only sorry that Pip wasn't there to enjoy it with her.

A week later, Marcy was looking with disbelief at the B plus inked on her senior thesis. The ground seemed to buckle under her feet and the features of the room around her seemed blanked out by white light. She was scarcely conscious of how she got out of the classroom. It is possible to walk quite a distance without conscious thought, and she was all the way out at the parking lot before she had even realized where she was going. She looked around at the parking lot full of cars, trying confusedly to remember where she had parked her own that morning, the morning that seemed years ago. She knew she had to get away. She needed to sit quietly somewhere and try to deal with the shock. She got in her car and drove home, cutting afternoon classes for the first time in her life.

At home, sitting at the dining-room table, she turned the pages of her thesis slowly, looking for some clue to what had gone wrong. She had misspelled *murmuring* and *niece*. But except for those red marks, the only comment was, "A bit dry and lifeless. Organization could be tightened."

Dry and lifeless? thought Marcy. The subject was Sumerian mythology. What did the woman expect, a rock video? If it was dry it was only because she had worked so carefully to make sure that every statement was supported by research. She had not gone off half-cocked, making vague statements about the significance of it all.

She was so angry it took her a long time to come to even that modest conclusion. Slowly, she became conscious of a cold fear in her stomach. This grade counted half of the semester's score in that class. Coupled with that weak unit test in May, it might bump her down to a B in the course. She dug up the folder of her old papers and figured up her English average. It was just as she had feared. She was two points away from an A.

She picked up the bound thesis and stared at it unseeingly. She was going to have to talk to Mrs. Lancaster, that was all. She was going to have to get this straightened out.

The following afternoon, sun streamed in the open windows of Room 301, but neither Marcy nor Mrs. Lancaster noticed.

"It wasn't up to your usual standard, Marcy. It was a very pedestrian treatment of the subject."

"It was a research paper. It was careful and not flashy."

"You'll remember I said the organization could be tightened up some, too. I notice the fertility gods were treated here on page ten and then again on page fourteen."

"In different contexts," Marcy countered.

"Grouping related subjects is a basic principle of organization. The transition here, too, I think is a bit clumsy." Mrs. Lancaster made a red squiggle by a short paragraph. "All in all, it was a good paper, a very good paper, but not the best."

Marcy was sure Pip Byron had gotten an A. It was obvious he was a favorite of Mrs. Lancaster's. She practically simpered when she called on him. Anything he did was just hunky-dory. Marcy spoke from between clenched teeth. "I'd like to see the grade book. I just want to see how the other grades run."

"I can't let you do that, Marcy. Of course, you may see your own grades, but I can't let you see other people's grades."

"But my own grade doesn't exactly have any meaning unless I see where it stands among all the others, does it?"

Mrs. Lancaster slapped her grade book closed. "I suggest you accept that this paper was not an example of your best work."

"Mrs. Lancaster, I worked as hard on that paper as I have ever worked on anything in my life. Every inch of it was meticulously written and buttressed by the most careful research. You could eat off of my footnotes! It was a beautiful piece of work."

"I'm afraid we aren't always the best judges of our own work. Lay this paper aside for a year or two and come back to it and I expect you will agree with me." Mrs. Lancaster rose. "I don't wish to cut you short, but I am already late for a faculty meeting."

The injustice left Marcy breathless. "I honestly do not think this is a B paper. I'd like a second opinion. I'd like to submit the paper to Mrs. MacLuhan and see what she would give it. If she gives it a B, too, then I'd be satisfied and let the subject rest."

"I can't agree to that, Marcy. Mrs. MacLuhan is not familiar with the Advanced Placement English curriculum so she is not in any position to give a judgment."

"You won't let Mrs. MacLuhan give her opinion on it?"

"Certainly not. That would be quite inappropriate. Now I really must go."

Marcy stood stock still while Mrs. Lancaster gathered up her belongings, as if by being still herself she could will Mrs. Lancaster to stay in the room and face her.

She didn't know whether to be insulted or outraged when Mrs. L. pointedly picked up her grade book to take with her when she left.

This was more than a difference of opinion about a grade, Marcy thought, feeling hot all over. It had all the looks of a conspiracy. Why was Mrs. Lancaster so keen to hide what was in her grade book? Why did she refuse to let an impartial teacher evaluate the paper? What was she hiding?

Walking slowly to her car, Marcy remembered the thousand dollar prize Byron Tobacco had given to Mrs. L. and decided that might be the explanation for what had happened. Mrs. L. had been paid off. Paid off openly in public under the cover of an education award. There had never been a Byron Tobacco Education award until this year, had there? Money, thought Marcy bitterly, can buy anything.

She had to go to her job directly after school, but that evening she called Sam.

"Sam? How'd you do on the senior thesis?"

"The usual, B. That's more or less what I figured. How about you?"

"B plus," Marcy spat. "Do you know what Pip got?"

"No. I know he put in a lot of work on it, though."

"I put in a lot of work on it, too! I slaved over that paper. All that talk of hers about research and footnotes and then at the last minute she does an about-face and acts like what she wants is some razzle-dazzle. I'd like to see a sample of her research. She probably doesn't know a good job when she sees one. Do you know I asked her if I could get a second opinion from Mrs. MacLuhan and she refused!"

"She did? I wonder why?"

"She gave me some junk about how Mrs. Mac-Luhan wasn't familiar with the AP English curriculum or something. It was pretty clear she was afraid of a second opinion. She wants to sit at that desk like some oriental potentate, while everybody kowtows. What really grates on me is the capriciousness of it. Why should a woman like that have any control over my future? Shouldn't she be accountable for what she does just like everybody else? If she were a doctor I could sue her for malpractice. If she were president of the United States I could take her to the Supreme Court. It's only because she's a teacher that she's got absolute power."

"Oh, Marce, I know just how you feel. Half the time I can't see any rhyme or reason in the grades. One time I'll kill myself and they'll hate it; another time I'll dash it off at the last minute and they're crazy about it."

Marcy doubted seriously that Sam understood how she felt but she put up with the expressions of sympathy in silence. There was no point in telling Sam her suspicions about the education award. She would only defend Pip and his family as usual.

"I remember when I turned in that outline for my history paper in Mr. Fisher's class," Sam was going on, "and I had worked so hard to get every line exactly parallel to the others the way he said and then he upped and marked me off for having complete sentences in it. And he hadn't said one word about not having complete sentences!"

"At least that didn't count half of your grade."

"True. Well, anyway, a B plus is very good on the thesis, Marce, considering what a hard grader Mrs. Lancaster is. You should be pretty pleased with that."

Pleased with it? Sam didn't know what it was like to strain every nerve and muscle for a major paper, to turn it in knowing it was an A paper and then to be slapped down. When Marcy hung up, she felt very alone.

Chapter Seven

Marcy could not quit thinking about the B she had been given on her senior thesis. Over and over she told Sam what Mrs. Lancaster had said and what she had said back. She knew that she was repeating herself, she knew that she was boring, but couldn't stop. Her mind was going in futile circles like a scratched record.

Seeing how distressed Marcy was, Sam felt angry. It wasn't fair. Marcy had put in an incredible amount of work on Mrs. Lancaster's course, and yet her complaint about the grade had been casually brushed off. Mrs. Lancaster hadn't really listened.

"Every grade can't be negotiable," Sam's dad protested when she broached the subject with him. "It would be a nightmare if you had to go through some complicated procedure for satisfying every student who didn't get the grade he expected."

"Marcy isn't just any student, and she wasn't just a little upset," Sam said stubbornly. "The senior thesis wasn't just any grade, either. It counted half of the grade for the course."

Sam didn't see why Mrs. L. couldn't have agreed to let Mrs. MacLuhan look at Marcy's thesis. Everyone knew there was a large subjective element in grading. In the interests of fairness, it made sense to let another teacher read a disputed paper. This business about Mrs. MacLuhan not being familiar with the AP English program was, to Sam's mind, a ridiculously fine scruple.

She felt that she finally understood why Luke and his mother had been fighting for years. Mrs. Lancaster might be one of the most respected teachers at the high school, but her integrity was the rigid kind that made Sam, for one, want to paste her one in the mouth.

Marcy's problem weighed on Sam and depressed her during the last couple of weeks of school. Sam had expected to enjoy those last days, but they weren't turning out at all the way she had hoped. She had thought seniors would be running through the halls hugging each other, crying sentimental tears and passing yearbooks around for people to sign with inane messages. But half the people she knew looked past her without seeing her, presumably wrapped up in their own worries. And it turned out that an amazing number of kids had not even bothered to order yearbooks. Sam's senior year was winding down with a fizzle.

The only stir of excitement occurred when invitations began arriving to a party Happy Chambers's parents were giving to celebrate Happy's graduation.

"They asked me to it," Marcy reported, surprised. "Did you get an invitation, too, Sam?"

"Sure. It's going to be a big party. That's why they're asking us. If they limited it to Happy's actual friends, it would have to be a very, very small party."

"A party of one, you mean."

"Everybody will be there."

"What you mean is everybody who is anybody will be there. Happy the snob—some things never change."

"It's nice of her parents, though, don't you think? It will be a lovely bash for us all. Happy told me they were going to have a seafood buffet and a band."

"They must have money to burn."

"Do you think people will dress up?"

"Sure. Toni Harkness is actually going to wear sequins. She told me."

"Toni Harkness would," said Sam.

There was certainly no doubt that the party, scheduled a week after graduation, excited more interest than anything else going on during the last week of school, certainly more than studying for exams. Two people asked Sam if she thought there would be dancing, and five reported breathlessly on Toni Harkness's decision to wear sequins.

The day before exams, seniors were issued mimeographed instructions on where to pick up and return their caps and gowns. Suddenly Sam was struck by a morbid fear that when her cap arrived it would be too small. She was certain she was fated to attend her own graduation looking like a clown. This fear was so silly, she hesitated to tell anyone about it. She wondered if it weren't a cover for some more sinister fear. Of not being ready to graduate, perhaps?

The final bits of school passed in such a haphazard, unexpected way, it was hard for Sam to realize that it was all over when she handed in her last exam. She had an odd at-sea feeling. She went to the rest room, combed her hair and restlessly redid some of the buttons on her shirt until it finally occurred to her that the dishevelment she felt was something of her mind and not her clothing.

"It's all behind us now," Pip said, as he drove Sam home from school that last day. "Papers, exams, the works. All done."

"Next stop, graduation." Sam brooded anxiously about the size of the cap she had ordered.

Pip watched the car's odometer flip over to an even ten thousand miles. "If we start now, we could be in Georgia by midnight."

Sam looked at him, startled. "Why are you all of a sudden talking about Georgia?"

"We could get married there without our parents signing for us. I looked it up. Blood test but no waiting period or consent for applicants over eighteen. By day after tomorrow we could be married."

Sam strained to hear the feeling behind his words. "It's as if you can't imagine any happy ending for us but getting married now."

"Maybe I can't."

"Why not? Don't you think people can go off and get to know other people and still come back to each other?"

"I don't know."

"I believe it happens. And if it doesn't, then it just isn't meant to be."

"Sam, if you know what you want, you should go after it and not sit around talking about what's 'meant to be.' I know what I want."

"You want to be married by some justice of the peace or something while your family is at home crying and saying you've gone out of your mind?"

"My parents eloped. They'd be in no shape to complain."

Realizing, at last, that what she was hearing under his words was fear, Sam reached for his hand. "It's going to be all right. We're going to be fine."

He squeezed her hand. "You promise?"

"Absolutely, cross my heart. No doubt about it."

"I can send you plane tickets to come up and see me, and I can fly down to see you. I can rent a car at the airport and drive over to Chapel Hill."

"We can see each other all the time. And we can talk on the phone, too."

"I could call you every Saturday night. If it were a regular thing like that, then I'd be sure of catching you in the dorm."

"That sounds like a good idea," Sam said. This was no time to argue the fine points. She could follow Pip's reasoning easily enough. If she were sitting around Saturday night waiting for him to call, she couldn't very well be out with another boy, could she?

By the time Pip dropped her off at her house, Sam could feel her own confidence seeping away. She went upstairs to her bedroom and stared out the window, uncertain what to do next, as if Pip's restlessness and unease had infected her. That talk about driving to Georgia had been vaguely disturbing. Was she doing the right thing? Pip was so smart. Was he right about this? Was she someday going to look back and be sorry that she had not run away with him to Georgia?

Impulsively, she dialed Luke's number. She remembered how driving around town with Luke shooting water guns at friends had lifted her spirits in the most amazing way. Dumb fun—that was what she needed. But though Luke's phone rang and rang, no one answered.

In the *Banner* office downtown Luke was leaning against the counter. He was watching an anemic-looking girl in the advanced stages of pregnancy stare fixedly at a computer monitor.

"See," Mr. Maxwell said proudly. "Any time a customer comes in and wants to run the same ad the next week, all Becky has to do is type in their phone number to bring up the ad. Show him the rate schedules, Becky. Couldn't be easier. After three days you'll be able to do it in your sleep."

Becky wiped her nose. "I have allergies," she sniffled. She pulled her cardigan sweater closer around her shoulders.

Luke looked around the room where seven or eight middle-aged women sat at their desks, heads bent over their work. All wore cardigan sweaters against the chill of the air conditioning. Most of them were so faded looking as to have no individual characteristics at all.

"Come on in back and I'll show you the time clock where you punch in," said Mr. Maxwell. "Now you're going to be able to start right after the fifteenth, right?

Actually, Becky's planning to stay on till the end of this month, so we probably aren't going to need you till the first."

Mr. Maxwell, a round, bald-headed little man, led Luke through a door into the somewhat livelier precincts behind the front office. Here people were moving between the desks, and bits of paper lay on the floor, smudged with footprints. Dirty coffee cups sat on the desks. Half-open doors revealed small untidy offices where piles of paper threatened to overflow off the desks and out the door. A plump man whose pants were shiny at the bottom thrust a memo onto a spindle and moved away to an office. A cave-chested girl with frizzy blond hair was studying a typed sheet. For Luke this scene was infused with an almost sacramental quality simply because it was a newspaper office. The smell of glue, dust and stale coffee was inextricably bound up in his mind with news over the wire. This office, he thought with reverence, is plugged into world events.

"I started out just the way you're starting out," Mr. Maxwell was saying. "Thirty years ago, in the classifieds. Of course, back then we didn't have computers. We did everything by hand. I was always waiting for my big chance. Kept praying an earthquake would strike Fenterville. I used to hope a presidential candidate would come through just on the off chance he'd get himself killed and give me my big chance. I didn't know when I was well off. These days I can appreciate the advantages of living in a peaceful town. We get our share of robberies and stabbings on Saturday night, of course, but we pick those up right off the police blotter. We don't really cover them.

Mostly we just cover town meetings and zoning disputes. Now, here's the time clock I was telling you about. We're planning to phase it out next year and convert to a fully computerized system. I expect that will be an unholy mess. There's such a thing as carrying this computer business too far.''

After Luke left the *Banner* office he had to walk to his car, which was parked on Howard Street. In the warm sunshine, he became unpleasantly aware of the clothes he was wearing. His stiff new tennis shoes had not yet taken on the glovelike feel of his old ones. The tag in his new shirt rubbed its sharp edge against the nape of his neck, and the pants were still stiff with sizing, a feel he hated. His family and friends had groused often enough about the state of his clothes that he had thought it wise to buy a completely new outfit for his visit to the *Banner* office, but moving in them now, he remembered what he hated about new clothes. Still, the effect looked spiffy enough. As he caught a glimpse of his reflection in a shop window, he was conscious of looking good.

He wondered if after years of working on the *Banner* he would fade to the same indeterminate milky hue of the other employees. Was that vague color the color of meekness and resignation? Did it seep out of your soul and permeate your body and even your clothes after years of punching a time clock? He shook his head and climbed into his car. If he weren't careful, he told himself, he was going to get moody and over-imaginative.

The next day, when Marcy got in from work, she lifted the mail out of the mailbox and carried it in to look over while she was getting supper started. Her mother had called to say they were having trouble reconciling the books at the bank and that she would be late.

As she tossed the mail onto the kitchen table, Marcy was startled to see a Lee High return address on one of the envelopes. She tore it open at once.

Dear Marcy:
This is to inform you that you will be salutatorian of this year's graduating class. You will need to meet with a committee of speech and English teachers ...

Marcy was too dazed to take in the rest of the letter.

Salutatorian? She was supposed to be valedictorian. She had had the highest grade point average in her class since the ninth grade. Everyone knew that.

Suddenly she realized that the B in English must have knocked her average down just below Pip Byron's. She had had no idea his average was so very close to hers.

When Marcy's mother got in from work, she was alarmed to find the apartment dark and Marcy lying in bed with a swollen and tear-streaked face.

"Sweetheart!" she cried. "Are you sick?"

Marcy blindly groped for the letter on her bedside table and held it out to her mother.

Her mother switched on the bedside lamp and read it in silence for a minute. "Oh, dear, are you sure this is right? I'd better call Mrs. Proctor tomorrow and try to find out what is going on."

"It's that B plus on the senior thesis," Marcy cried. "You remember, it counted half the grade. That B in English must have knocked me down below Pip. I had no idea our averages were that close. They must have had to carry it out to the hundredths place for one letter grade to make the difference!"

Her mother sat down on the bed and patted her shoulder awkwardly. "My poor little baby, I know this is a disappointment."

"Disappointment!" choked Marcy. "What about the Rotary Scholarship that goes to the valedictorian? What about the money I need if I'm going to go to Stanford?"

"I'm sure we can work out something, sweetheart. Maybe I can get a—a bank loan or something."

Marcy cast a look at the squalid gloom of the bedroom and rolled over to bury her face in her pillow, choking with sobs. What idiot would give them credit? They could barely pay their bills as it was. Her mother's flaky optimism was almost more heartbreaking than the grim reality. It was so pathetic.

The hardest thing to bear, Marcy thought, would be the sympathy of her friends. She was going to have to tell them, but not just yet. She would wait until she felt a little stronger.

While her mother fixed dinner, Marcy lay in bed, staring at the letter and feeling sick and hollow. She wondered if this was the way people felt when they lost a finger in an accident, this feeling that from this moment on everything was changed, ruined.

Looking at the letter again, she noticed that the first meeting with the speech and English teachers was the day after tomorrow. Mrs. Lancaster would be there to criticize her speech and make suggestions. What an irony! The idea of that woman sitting smugly at a desk, commenting on the organization and the delivery of the salutatory speech filled Marcy with rage. And yet there was nothing she could do. No matter how smart she was or how hard she worked, in the end, it seemed, they could take it all away from her. The teacher and the establishment had all the power, and she had none.

Marcy's mother stuck her head in the door. "Come on in and get something to eat, sweetheart. You've got to keep up your strength, you know. You'll feel better if you get up and get your mind off all this."

If that ridiculous statement had not come from her own mother, Marcy would have considered it an attempt at sick humor. A person did not work four years for something and lose it only to have her mind taken off it by a lamb chop.

At Sam's house, Pip had just phoned. "Sam, guess what? The darnedest thing!"

"What? Tell me. Is it something good?"

"I'll say. A letter from the school was waiting for me when I got home. I'm going to be valedictorian!"

"You're what?"

"You heard me—valedictorian. Marcy must have stumbled at the last minute."

"The B on the senior thesis," Sam groaned.

"Is that what it was? I knew we were really close but I knew her grades have always been incredibly consistent so I didn't really expect this. It's really something, isn't it? I can't wait to tell my father. He's going to love it. It's unbelievable to have it fall into my lap like this at the last minute. All this time I've been kicking myself for taking band tenth and eleventh grade. You see, by the time it hit me that band was an unweighted credit and that an A in band was actually pulling my average down, the damage was done. But now it turns out it didn't matter after all. Let's face it, salutatorian is okay, but this is better. It's not as if you can go around the rest of your life explaining you were just one decimal point away from the person on top. It's better just to *be* the person on top. Are you okay, Sam? You seem awfully quiet. You are happy for me, aren't you?"

"I was just thinking what a blow this is going to be for Marcy."

"Yeah, I guess so. But you don't mind if I don't dwell on that right now, do you?"

"Oh, I'm sorry, Pip! Of course, it's great for you. You must be just—ecstatic."

"I'm feeling pretty good, all right. Want to go out and celebrate with me? Mom and Dad are at some political fund-raiser, Terry's spending the night at a friend's house and I'm sort of a one-person parade with nowhere to go."

"Sure! I'd love to celebrate with you."

After Sam hung up, she groaned. When Marcy heard the news she was going to be in bad shape. Sam felt she ought to stand by to hold her hand. But how could she have told Pip to go celebrate by himself?

She went upstairs, put on panty hose and pulled her blue crepe out of the closet. When she turned to her mirror to smooth on a smidgen of eye shadow, her finger felt icy against her face. Obviously, her anxiety had spread even to the tips of her fingers. She wondered if Marcy picked up her mail yet. When she pictured Marcy opening the envelope, Sam got a clutching feeling in her stomach. Why did Pip have to go and be valedictorian?

Downstairs the kitchen door slammed. Her parents were back from getting groceries. Sam ran down in her stocking feet to give them the news.

"Oh, dear," said her mother. "Poor Marcy."

"When it's that close," Sam's father said, "I think they ought to have joint valedictorians. It's not as if grading is an exact science."

"You can say that again!" said Sam, thinking of Mrs. Lancaster's B on the thesis.

"One letter grade in one course simply isn't a statistically significant difference," her father went on. "To make a big deal out of it is absurd. In fact, I don't see why we have to have a valedictorian and salutatorian at all. Is it really so important to have a grade average a few points higher than your classmates?"

"How is Marcy taking it?" asked her mother.

"I don't know. She hasn't called."

"You could call her," suggested her mother.

Sam grabbed hold of a kitchen chair, shaken at the very idea. "And risk being the one to tell her?" she breathed in horror.

"Poor Marcy," said her dad. He took out a couple of cans of soup and put them on the counter, then suddenly noticed Sam's dress. "What are you all dressed up for, Sam? Are you going someplace?"

"I'm going out to celebrate with Pip."

"Oh, dear," said her mother. She put the milk in the refrigerator. "You're in a rather delicate situation aren't you? Having to rejoice with the winner and condole with the loser.''

"The thing is, Mom, it's not Pip's fault that he got valedictorian, and naturally he's really happy about it. Well, who wouldn't be? But as a matter of fact, it is a little bit hard for me to be very enthusiastic because I keep thinking of Marcy's feelings. I mean, she had counted on it! Everybody has known for years that she would be valedictorian!''

"Poor Marcy," said her father again.

The doorbell rang. "That's Pip," gasped Sam. "I've got to run upstairs and get my shoes. Now don't tell him what we've been talking about, okay? I mean, just congratulate him. Smile and all that." Sam threw the swinging door open and prepared to sprint upstairs. "Oh, and if Marcy calls while I'm gone, *don't* tell her I'm out with Pip, okay? Tell her I've, uh, gone to the library. No, she might come over there looking for me. Tell her you don't know where I am. No, she wouldn't believe that. Maybe you'd better just not answer the phone, maybe that's the thing. Golly, aren't you two ever going to answer the door? Pip's waiting! And remember what I said!" Sam bolted through the dining room and tore upstairs.

When she came out of her room a few minutes later, Pip was standing at the foot of the stairs with her parents. He had obviously just been receiving their hearty congratulations. As Sam ran down the stairs she hoped their remarks had sounded genuine enough.

"We won't be too late," he was saying. "We're just going out to dinner. Uh, of course, the service is pretty slow and we won't exactly rush when we're finished. No school tomorrow and everything."

Sam had no difficulty in interpreting these slightly disjointed remarks. Pip had suddenly realized midstream that he wanted to leave some time for them to park somewhere without having to worry about Sam's parents calling out the highway patrol because they were late.

They walked down the porch steps together. "You look sleek," Sam said. "Like some panther on a tree branch surveying six million tons of gazelle meat on the hoof."

"You've got it. That's the way I feel, as if the whole world were mine for the taking. Crazy isn't it? The world's the same as it was yesterday, but all of a sudden I'm on top of it."

Suddenly he grabbed both her hands and swung her around. They went round and round in the front yard until she was dizzy and they were both laughing and breathless.

She put her hands on his shoulders and grinned at him. "You are crazy."

"I feel awfully good. Maybe you're right. Maybe that is crazy."

Suddenly Sam felt embarrassed by their happiness and let her hands drop to her sides. She was anxious to get into the car where there would be no chance Marcy might drive by and see them.

Pip threw the car door open for her and got in on the other side. "It's good to graduate with a bang. I suppose on some level it must have bothered me a lot to come in second to Marcy or I wouldn't be floating like this now. You think it's some unreconstructed male-chauvinist part of me? Or maybe just knowing how she has all this contempt for me? Or I guess it could be that I just like to win like you said. Anyway, it doesn't matter now. I've got it. And it feels fantastic!''

Although the weather was fine, Pip had put the car's top up so Sam's hair wouldn't get messed up on the way to dinner. "This is the part where in old-time musicals the hero burst into song," he said.

"And orchestra music miraculously appears whether they're in a hayfield or the streets of Paris or whatever."

"I tell you, Sam, sometimes I wonder what I've done to be so blipping happy."

"You work hard."

"Yeah, but the best things were just handed to me—you, my parents. Even, I guess, my brain—such as it is. Heck, I'm not going to sit here feeling guilty about it. What's the point of not getting a kick out of it? If I didn't it would all be wasted, right? And it's g-reat! Absolutely out of this world."

As twilight gathered among the trees, the white Mercedes slid smoothly toward the outskirts of town. When it pulled up in front of La Petite Marmite, Pip said doubtfully, "I hope you aren't getting tired of this place, Sam. You know how it is, it's either here or burgers. Unless you want Chinese. Want to try Chinese for a change? Or we could drive out to Silver Lake, but that's another fifteen miles."

"Oh, no. I like this place. We've had some happy times here, haven't we?" Sam could feel herself tearing up. How many times would they come here again? Maybe never.

Pip put his arms around her and pulled her close to him. They clung together. "Jeez, I am lucky," he said thickly. "So lucky. And I know it, too."

At first Sam couldn't think why she felt sad. It was as if a minor strain of music were playing somewhere in her head. Then she remembered Marcy.

Chapter Eight

The following week Marcy and Pip were in Room 305 together. So far Marcy had carefully avoided looking at Pip. They had just finished reading their prepared speeches to their assembled audience of speech and English teachers and were waiting for the final comments.

Mr. Lindstrom sat with crossed legs, tapping a pencil against the sole of his shoe. "As you know, people, this is the last practice before the ceremony, but I think you're both in good shape. You've incorporated our suggestions very nicely." He cocked an interrogatory head toward the other teachers. "Ladies? Any further comments?"

Mrs. Lancaster took off her glasses. "Marcy, when you announce your theme with that first word, you aren't pausing enough for emphasis. It should go,

'Friendship' pause pause. Perhaps as much as three seconds' pause. That's a good opportunity for you to establish eye contact with the audience, as well.''

''Just don't lose your place while you're busy establishing eye contact,'' warned Mr. Lindstrom. ''One year our valedictorian let a page of his speech slip down off the podium and couldn't figure out what had happened to it!''

Mrs. MacLuhan, a small restless woman, was running her fingers through her thick curly hair. ''Pip, I don't know what it is, but I feel something is lacking. I mean, it's perfect, brilliant. But can't you try for more, uh, warmth? I don't know, the human touch maybe. Ernie, what do you think? Eloise?''

''It sounded fine to me,'' said Mrs. Lancaster.

Naturally, thought Marcy bitterly. Anything Pip does is fine.

''Honestly, I think this late in the game Pip might be safer sticking to his natural delivery. Any more comments, people? No? Well, let me just say that I think these are both admirable speeches, and I'm sure I speak for everyone when I say we expect to be very proud of you.''

Marcy jumped up out of her seat and fled the room.

Luke was parked near the administration building waiting for her.

''How'd it go?'' he asked, as she got into his old green car.

''Fine.''

''You want to talk about it?''

''Not really.''

"I guess they were full of the usual supercilious comments and bad advice. You're probably better off trusting your own instincts."

"I intend to," she said. She looked grim.

Luke drove out of the parking lot. "Look, Marce, you want to get a hammer and we'll drive to a junk yard and you can trash some old cars or something?"

"It's okay. I'm holding myself together."

"Maybe holding yourself together isn't good. Maybe you ought to scream and yell some."

"I've already done all that. I'll be all right, Luke."

"So, you want to go get something to eat?"

"Okay."

"You know Carolina and Wake Forrest are both good schools. Is there anything so bad about staying around near here where you can come home sometime and we can see each other?"

"No, of course not. I mean, I'd like to be able to see you. It's just that you know I had my heart set on Stanford." She stared out the window. What bothered him was that she had the blank expression of someone looking out the window of a bus. It was as if she had forgotten he was there.

"Marce, I feel like you're a million miles away. Hey, Earth calling Marcy! Can you read me?"

She flushed. "I'm sorry. I guess I'm not over the shock of it." A tear streaked her face, and Luke pulled the car over to the side of the road and took her in his arms while she buried her face against him and cried hot tears onto the shoulder of his shirt.

"Look," he said. "Have you thought about just skipping graduation? There's no law that says you've got to go through with this junk. Who cares what anybody thinks? You're probably never going to see any of these jerks again anyway, right?''

"Skip graduation?" she said. Her red-rimmed eyes widened with astonishment. "I wouldn't miss it for the world!"

Luke winced. It looked as if he were going to have to go so as to stand by Marcy. When he thought of the pious sentiments, the flags with gold fringes, the rows of meek graduates in folding chairs and the droning voices that would inevitably be a part of the event, it was all he could do not to groan out loud. "Okay," he said, "if that's what you want to do."

The afternoon of the graduation ceremony was quite hot and a large number of the graduates were wearing shorts under their black gowns. The rumor went around that Toni Harkness was wearing nothing at all under hers, but Sam did not believe it. Standing on the thin and heavily trodden grass of the parking lot of the stadium, kids were zipping up their black gowns and awkwardly adjusting their caps. Sam didn't want to spoil the careful angle at which she had finally got her own cap arranged but she kept nervously fingering her gold tassel and pulling it off center. The gold tassel indicated she was in the upper ten percent of her class; all other graduates had black tassels. The seniors were to be lined up in order of their grade point averages. Once Sam would have taken pleasure in having achieved such a respectable position because she was well aware that some people didn't think much of her brains and it was nice to surprise them by not being at the bottom of the class. But lately she was getting disgusted with the emphasis on grades.

Because of the confusion around her, she only caught glimpses of her friends in the most haphazard way. All the kids around her had been familiar faces in her life, most of them since the early years of grade school. How odd to think this was the last time she would be seeing many of them.

Luke came up looking flat-headed in his black mortarboard. He was wearing a pair of tennis shoes so ancient that his big toe was in imminent danger of breaking through the worn canvas.

He ran a finger around the inside of his collar. "Jeez," he said. "This heat is not to be believed. I hope they've got ambulances standing by for the poor suckers who pass out."

"It could have been worse. It could have rained and we'd all be stuffed into the auditorium. How's Marcy holding up?"

"I don't know. She had to get here early because she's going to be up on the platform, and naturally she came with her mother. Heck, I don't know why I say 'naturally.' I sure didn't come with my mother. We're not even speaking now. Did you hear that Toni Harkness is naked under her gown? That girl's got the right idea. Wish I had thought of it. Uh-oh, they're already lining people up. You better get moving, Sam. You're a lot closer to the front of the line than I am."

Sam scurried up to where Mr. Lindstrom stood with a clipboard. "Davis, Lutisha!" he bellowed. "Right here, Lutisha. Stand right there and don't budge. Horton, Melanie! Stand right behind Lutisha, Melanie. Cut it out, you guys. You want to get your diplomas or not? All right then, make an effort to behave like adults, okay?''

Slowly a snaking line took shape, kept in order by Mr. Lindstrom's assistants who were posted at intervals down the extent of the line. Sam was astonished to find herself placed directly behind Happy. What an irony that this day should find her standing next to her oldest enemy.

''Watch it,'' said Happy. ''You almost touched my mortarboard. I had it put on at the hairdresser this afternoon and I don't want it to get moved out of place.''

Sam controlled her worst instincts, which were to tip the cap off of Happy's head with a cackle of wild laughter. ''You mean, you've been going around all afternoon with that thing on your head?''

''I thought that was better than looking stupid at my own graduation,'' said Happy, looking meaningfully at Sam's cap. The line surged confusedly, and Happy snapped at the boy ahead of her. ''Would you watch where you're going for a change, Harry? I mean, do you mind? Those shoes are a hundred percent kid, imported from Italy.''

''Yes, your majesty.''

Inside the stadium, the band struck up *''Gadeamus Igatur''*.

''This is it!'' said Happy, grabbing for Sam's shoulder. Sam recoiled, but before she could detach Happy's hands the girl burst into tears. ''We're actually graduating,'' Happy sobbed. ''We'll never see each other again!''

The idea of never seeing Happy again cheered Sam up so much she was able to pat her on the shoulder.

Sam even hiked up her black gown and fished her handkerchief out of her pocket and offered it to Happy. "All our friends," Happy sobbed into the handkerchief. "We'll never see them again."

"We'll see each other at your party next weekend," Sam reminded her.

"Move along," whispered one of Mr. Lindstrom's assistants. "Move steadily and watch the person in front of you. Be careful not to step on anybody's gown when you sit down. Move it, kids. This is it!"

"Golly, it's so—so final," sobbed Happy, wiping her eyes.

Sam gave her a discreet push, and soon they were actually filing into the stadium. Sam saw Pip and Marcy sitting stiffly side by side next to the dignitaries on the platform. Sam gave them a little wave as the graduates approached the folding chairs, but they didn't seem to see her.

When all the seniors were seated on the folding chairs arranged in front of the bleachers, Luke was several rows behind Sam. Flashbulbs were popping all over the stadium, and a number of fathers with video cameras had positioned themselves just behind the graduates. Luke was bracing himself for an hour of boredom. He saw Happy dabbing at her eyes with a handkerchief and wondered what on earth she was crying about. She was probably sick not to have one more chance to get her talons in anybody before she left. He seemed to remember hearing she was going to some ritzy girls' school in the East, but he wasn't sure about that. He hadn't seen much of her since he had gotten kicked off the newspaper staff.

Everyone stood up while the band played "The Star-Spangled Banner." Then they had to remain standing for the school song. Luke could feel sweat trickling down his leg. When at last they were allowed to sit down, the droning of the voices from the platform began. Toni Harkness twisted around to look for her boyfriend, and Luke spotted a flash of white at the neck of her gown. Regretfully he decided that Toni was not naked under her gown after all. Too bad. In his opinion, much of the tedium of otherwise hopeless ceremonies could have been relieved by nudity. In fact, if even the speakers came to graduation buck naked, that alone would probably cut the pomposity level of the speeches by half, not to mention that it would probably cut the length of the speeches, and on a hot day like this everybody would have been a lot more comfortable. The sun seemed to soak into the black fabric of his gown, and his forehead was damp under the ridiculous hat. He fervently wished he were at the beach.

After a while he realized that Marcy had risen and was going to the podium. He knew he would have to listen to this part carefully because the chances were she would ask him about how the speech had sounded.

Marcy's voice sounded clearly over the stadium, echoing slightly.

"I know you all thought that I was going to be your valedictorian. Until a few days ago, I thought so myself. But thanks to a well-financed campaign by some of the major powers of this town, someone else will have that honor this afternoon.

"I don't believe it's any secret that my English teacher, Mrs. Lancaster, has her favorites. But even though I knew this, I was shocked to be given a grade on my senior thesis that was lower than any I have ever gotten in English. Mrs. Lancaster refused to let another teacher look at my paper. She refused to let me see any of the other grades in the class. It was almost as if she had something to hide. I was puzzled until I remembered the large cash award given her by Byron Tobacco Company. Is it simply coincidence that Pip Byron was more lucky in the scoring of his senior thesis? I think not."

Luke, suddenly cold with shock, was staring up at Marcy as if he had never seen her before. She was standing up in front of three thousand people and saying his mother had been paid off! He saw the assistant principal get up from his seat and fumble with a knob on the microphone, but the fellow's mechanical abilities did not seem to be up to the task of turning it off.

Sam's hands were clutched to her chest. She thought she had quit breathing entirely, and her eyes flickered anxiously from Marcy's face to Pip's. She had seen Pip slowly become rigid, his feet together, his dark eyes fixed on Marcy. It was as if a curtain had come down on his face. Sam thought that she would never forgive Marcy. Oblivious and white-faced at the podium, Marcy went on in a clear voice.

"This was only the final act of a campaign that began two years ago when grades transferred to

Lee from another school were given special treatment in order to make the other candidate's average more competitive. What pressure, what influence was brought to bear on that occasion, I cannot say. Only one thing is clear to me this afternoon—it is sad indeed when the power and influence of money reach even into the field of learning. It is my loss, yes, but it is everyone else's loss as well."

Marcy then gathered her notes together and calmly walked off the platform. The audience was buzzing in confusion but no one stopped her as she walked down the steps and out of the stadium.

Pip slowly rose to his feet and moved over to the podium. Sam did not know what to expect, whether Pip would try to defend himself or whether he would throw down his notes and leave. Anything seemed possible in this emotionally charged atmosphere with all the pinched and appalled faces on the platform turned toward him. When he began to speak, the buzzing audience fell silent. To Sam, who knew him so well, his voice sounded as strangely detached as if it were coming from a tape recorder. "The world we know is so fraught with complexities," he began, "that we may at times feel paralyzed into inaction."

Sam sighed. The words had a strange appropriateness in the circumstances, but she recognized the opening line of his prepared speech. He was going on as if nothing had happened. After all, what choice did he have, really? Maybe he felt he had to do what he could to keep the graduation ceremony from falling apart. Or perhaps he scarcely knew what he was doing

and was only frantically clinging to what was familiar.

When he finished his speech and sat down, the stadium again began to buzz, and Sam realized that the
more alert people were probably explaining what had
gone on to the less informed and less attentive people
sitting near them. After all, the salutatory speech had
been short, and Sam could believe that to someone less
familiar with the facts of the case, it might have been
hard to follow Marcy's accusations.

Not surprisingly, the rest of the ceremony seemed
like an anticlimax. After the salutatorian has de-
nounced the valedictorian and accused a member of
the faculty of being on the take, everything that fol-
lows is bound to seem a bit tame.

Sam went up with the rest of the students in her turn
to get her diploma, but the whole thing seemed irrel-
evant compared to the human drama unfolding
around her. What was she going to say to Pip? How
was she ever going to face Marcy? Someone, she noticed, had been quick-witted enough to pull Marcy's
diploma from the stack so that her absence would not
be accented when her name was called. Sam's damp
fingertips stuck to her furled diploma, and when she
got back to her seat she wiped them on her gown.
Then in a final burst of sententiousness and music, the
ceremony was over.

Sam looked around frantically for Pip. People were
gathering in small groups all over the stadium, taking
snapshots. Behind her she heard a man saying, "Good
for her! She sure told 'em." He added in a lower voice,
"Of course, she'll regret it the rest of her life."

Then Sam saw Pip. He was coming down from the platform holding his diploma and looking dazed. She ran over to him and grabbed his hand. "Oh, Pip!" she cried. "I know it was awful. I know just how you must feel."

He looked down at her with burning eyes. "You do? Someone has stood in front of three thousand people and called *you* a crook?" He wrenched away from her. She watched his retreating back for a second in dismay and then ran after him.

The Byrons and Sam's own parents were converging on them from the stands. Mrs. Byron was beautiful in a large-brimmed black hat, the highest of heels and a chic dress with small black polka dots, but her mouth was working in distress. Mr. Byron, graying at the temples and with beads of sweat on his forehead, looked grave. "What a disaster," Pip's father exclaimed. "Unbelievable! Sam, did you have any idea this was going to happen?"

"Golly, no! Not a clue! I mean, I knew Marcy was upset but I thought her speech was going to be about friendship!"

Pip snorted.

Sam suspected her parents would have reached them first had they not been delayed by her father's colleagues babbling about Marcy's speech. All the teachers had been seated together directly behind the graduates.

Sam's mother came up fanning her face with her program. "Pip, I'm so sorry your happy day had to have this blight on it. Sam, did you have any suspicion Marcy was going to do this?"

"No, no, a thousand times no! Why do people keep asking me that? How could I know? I didn't have a clue!"

Sam's father put his hand on her shoulder. "Calm down, kiddo. This has been a pretty grueling afternoon for all of us. I'm afraid poor Eloise is going to need mouth-to-mouth resuscitation. The only thing holding her up when I left was all the colleagues crowding around her."

"Eloise?" frowned Mr. Byron. "Who is Eloise?"

"She's the one you were supposed to have paid off, Dad," said Pip bitterly. "Don't you remember?"

Sam heard Mr. Byron's sharp intake of breath. "And that's all I need! Can't you see the newspaper story? Byron Buys Valedictory for Son."

"It hasn't exactly been a picnic for me, either, you know," said Pip coldly.

Mrs. Byron dabbed at her eyes. Terry stood silent at her side, looking at Pip with big, frightened eyes.

"I don't know about the rest of you, but I'm getting out of this place," said Pip. "I just hope my car's not blocked in."

"I'm going with you," Sam said. Pip's mother shot her a grateful look. Sam supposed she didn't like the idea of Pip's driving off by himself in a black rage.

By the time Sam and Pip reached the Mercedes, the cars around his had thinned out some. Pip bumped down over the curb to the street. "I suppose you know that all those people back there believed every word of what she said."

"Oh, no. You're wrong. I didn't believe it. My parents didn't. The idea of Mrs. Lancaster selling grades is absolutely absurd! Nobody could believe it!"

"So, you think my dad would offer the bribe, you just don't think she would take it. Is that right?"

"That's not what I meant at all."

"It's pretty clear to me where everybody's sympathy is going to lie. Here's Marcy, working part-time, living in a dump, struggling valiantly, and here am I, a guy who wasn't even born around here, an outsider, for Pete's sake." He snorted. "Who's going to believe Marcy's lying? How can I even prove it if I set out to? Mrs. L. got that education prize, Marcy got the B on the thesis. How can anybody prove there isn't any connection? Besides, I'll bet you we never even get the chance to try. Sue her for slander? The idea's laughable. The thing is, Sam, no matter what I did, it would look nasty and vindictive, even if I could prove she's lying. Jeez, what could have possessed her?"

Sam had a pretty good idea of the kind of feelings that had moved Marcy to lash out. But she was sensitive enough to know it would be a mistake to try to outline Marcy's point of view to Pip right now.

"Nobody's ever going to forget this," Pip said bitterly. "People will be fanning out all over the state, taking this story with them. Whenever my name comes up somebody will whisper that my father bought my grades for me."

He pulled up at a light and looked over at her. "Sam, you really didn't know she was going to do this?"

"How can you think I would know something like that and not make a move to stop her!"

"I don't know. I guess I'm feeling so beleaguered, I'm not sure who I can trust."

Sam grabbed his free hand and held on tight.

Chapter Nine

Sam and Pip parked out by Crow's Falls, and Pip stared at the falls for several minutes. Finally, he spoke. "Well, you're on my side, anyway."

"Of course, I am!"

"I'll bet all over town right now people are probably saying 'Poor Marcy.' I can hear it—loud choruses of 'Poor Marcy.' She could run me down with a truck, and people would say, 'What was he doing standing in the middle of the street?'"

"It doesn't matter what people think."

"Sam, this is where I live! This is where my little sister goes to school. This is where my father was hoping to run for public office!"

"I think Marcy's temporarily insane about not getting that Rotary Scholarship. I think that's what was going on with her."

"What?"

"The Rotary Scholarship goes to the valedictorian. Marcy needed it to go to Stanford, and she really had her heart set on it."

"Look, excuse me, but as a victim, I'm not much interested in her motives. Jeez, all those practice sessions where she went and read that speech about friendship! The deceit! Look, Sam, if she needed that scholarship—and this is the first I've heard about it—why didn't she come to me and tell me so? Dad could probably have fixed it so it would go to Marcy in default of my taking it."

"She wouldn't do that."

"No, she'd rather cut me and my whole family down in front of half of the town, wouldn't she?"

"Nobody wants to be a beggar, and Marcy's really sensitive about being poor."

"She's mean-spirited, vindictive, coldhearted, hateful and she didn't bother to check out any of her so-called facts." Pip pushed his hands against the steering wheel. "And that's my most charitable opinion. I suppose the rest of my life when I see people on a street corner whispering, I'm going to think they're talking about this. To think I was trying to get my Posada grandparents to come down for the big day!" He shuddered. "I'm just glad they couldn't make it."

Sam stroked his hair and murmured scarcely intelligible words of comfort. After a while she could feel his rigid body beginning to untighten, and she ventured to lightly kiss his earlobe.

"I guess next you're going to tell me that someday I'll look back on this and laugh."

"Well, no," Sam conceded. "I wouldn't go that far."

They sat quietly for a while, watching the falls, their arms around each other. Finally, Pip said, "I guess I better take you home and get on home myself. My family's probably having a council of war. I don't know what Dad's going to want to do. I expect he's talking to a lawyer or something."

When Pip dropped Sam off at her house, she was surprised to see that no one was home. Only Fruitcake, the family beagle, greeted her. After a few excited barks, Fruity lay down panting in front of the big fan sitting on the floor of the kitchen. Sam poured herself a glass of iced tea. She felt wrung out.

Her parents came in a few minutes later.

"Where've you been?" asked Sam.

"We thought we'd better go over to the Lancasters' and express our support for Eloise."

Her mother kicked off her dress shoes and stood in front of the kitchen fan, legs apart, letting the air blow through the thin fabric of her skirt. "If the Byrons ever bribe you, Larry, let's put the money into air conditioning."

"Don't even joke about something like that. Poor Eloise, Teacher of the Year, and now this! Really, the last person anyone would believe would be up to anything shady! You should have seen her, Sam. She was reeling from the blow."

Sam's mother pulled a quart jar of iced tea out of the refrigerator. "I saw you talking to Luke, Larry. Did he have any idea this was going to happen?"

"He says not."

Sam was struck with a wave of remorse. She had forgotten all about how awful this would be for Luke. To have the girl he loved accuse his mother of being a crook—nothing could put a person in a worse bind than that. "Has Luke talked to Marcy at all?"

Her father poured some ice into a glass. "I don't think so. He probably came straight home from the graduation with his parents. If it were possible for Luke to look bad, I'd say he looked awful. I really think it was as much of a shock to him as to anyone. He seemed to be struck dumb."

Sam's mother put her glass on the table and sat down. "What Marcy must have been suffering to be driven to do this!"

"There's the social worker mentality, for you," said Sam's dad wryly. "Can you spare a little sympathy for my colleague whose reputation has been so casually destroyed? Imagine if some kid had gone up there and accused me of being on the take!"

"I know, dear. It is awful for Eloise. And for Pip and the Byrons, too. But you don't expect seventeen- and eighteen-year-old kids to act with the self-control of adults. Marcy's been driving herself to make those high grades for years. To expect that she can give up what she's been aiming for all these years and be a good sport about it—well, don't you think that's expecting too much of someone who's so young?"

Sam's father glanced at the kitchen clock. "What a day! And what an unholy mess! Have you forgotten we're supposed to go to the Fergusons' tonight, Ginny?"

"Yikes! I had forgotten. And I'm going to have to go up and shower. I'm dripping with sweat. Sam, can you get your own dinner? I hate to leave you like this, but we couldn't turn down the Fergusons again. It was starting to look pointed.''

"I may go over and get Luke to go for hamburgers with me. He's probably ready to get out of the house."

"Good idea," said her father. "When I last saw him, he looked like he was going under for the third time."

Sam called ahead so Luke would be watching for her, and when she drove up he came out. A number of cars were parked in the driveway and in front of the house. It looked almost as if the Lancasters were having a party.

"You don't want to go in," Luke muttered as he climbed in her car. "Everybody's coming by to give their condolences. It's gruesome. And let's go someplace that has a drive-through window. I don't exactly feel like running into anybody."

Sam drove slowly out of the neighborhood and headed toward Sunset Avenue. "Have you talked to Marcy?"

"What would I say? Sam, do you think she really believes all that stuff she said?"

"I guess she must. But she never said anything to me. Of course, I knew she wasn't happy with the way Pip's grades were transferred from that private school, because she got her aunt to write that letter to the newspaper about it, and I think she even lodged a complaint with the administration. And of course I knew she was really upset about that B your mother gave her. We all knew that. But she never said anything to me about the education prize being a bribe.

Of course, now that I think about it, she wouldn't. She'd expect me to take Pip's side.''

"How's Pip taking it? Honest, for the first time, the very first time, I actually felt sorry for the guy."

"Oh, Luke, what she did to him was just awful. Looking at him up there, I felt as if he were turning to stone before my eyes. He's not the kind to laugh off an attack like that. He's really hurting. It's so unfair!''

"Tell me about it! What about my mother? My father's saying she ought to ask to go before the school board and make a statement. They're talking about canceling their Grand Canyon vacation so she can be here next week when the school board meets."

"You didn't have the slightest clue that Marcy was going to do this?''

"Why do people keep asking me that? It's pretty clear Marcy doesn't care what I think or she wouldn't have stood up there in front of God and everybody and accused my mother of being a criminal. Do you know Mom actually asked how I could possibly believe that of her. She asked me! As if I were some collaborator in the whole thing, as if Marcy and I were joined at the head or something. Honestly, Sam, I was so appalled I could hardly get out the words to deny it. 'Do I look like somebody who knew what was going on?' I said. 'Do you really think I'd let her do something like that without saying a word to warn you?' Heck, I was as surprised as anybody.''

Sam sighed. ''You know, the really awful thing is I can sort of see how it looked to Marcy. I couldn't say that to Pip, of course, but I could see how it would all add up in her mind, feeling the way she did. She just came up with the wrong conclusion, that's all. It was pretty courageous of her to take on the administration and the richest family in town right out in public that way. Nobody could say she doesn't have guts. It's just that she was wrong, all wrong.''

"Don't give me that. I'm living in the same house as the wounded. What kind of nerve does it take to blast somebody who can't talk back? You know what really bothers me?'' Luke's voice sank until it was scarcely audible. "When I think of some of those things I said about my mother. You know, about how I didn't have any respect for her and how she didn't have any scruples? I mean, it's no secret we've had our problems, but she'd never do anything really wrong! She's laughably honest! The way I've been dumping on my mother all this time, maybe Marcy felt like she had a license to go after her. Maybe she thought I wouldn't even care.'' He shot Sam an anguished look.

Sam wouldn't have been surprised if there was something to what Luke had said, but she didn't think it would be kind to agree. "Oh, everybody complains about their family, Luke. Nobody thinks anything about it. You know, we can all dump on our own family but we don't want anybody else to. That's pretty standard.''

"Yes, but—''

"I doubt if Marcy was thinking much at all. She got so mad and upset she didn't really think about the consequences. Revenge just blotted out everything else.''

"Well, she sure didn't expect you and me to come and throw our arms around her afterwards, did she?''

"She's going away to college pretty soon," Sam said sadly. "I guess she figured what we thought didn't matter that much."

Luke ran his fingers through his hair. "I can't believe this is happening to me." Over his cheekbones, his fair skin was faintly flushed with distress.

"What are you going to say if Marcy calls you?"

"You've got to be kidding, Sam. Marcy's not going to call my house. And risk getting my mother?"

"I guess you're right."

"And I'm not going to call her, either. Believe me."

While Luke and Sam were driving to Wendy's, Marcy was on the phone talking to Toni Harkness.

"Man, it, like, blew me away!" Toni was saying. "I said to Benji, 'How did she have the nerve?' You really told 'em, Marcy. I've got to give you credit. You didn't sit there and take it lying down."

"I guess I was pretty angry."

"Everybody knew you were supposed to be valedictorian. We all knew it. They'd already put it in the yearbook, even. The nerve of those people, messing around with the grades like that. Those rich kids think they can get away with anything."

"Well, I appreciate your support, Toni. Thanks for calling."

"Yeah, anytime. Hey, go to it, tell 'em how it is. That's what I say."

Marcy's mother came out of the kitchen with a glass of iced water. "Are you going to change before we go over to Hilda's, sweetheart?"

Marcy felt drained from all the excitement. When she remembered the long walk down from the platform and out of the stadium, her knees still felt weak. Luckily she had never doubted her mother's support. Sarah McNair was not possessed of much courage. She might have tried to stop Marcy if she had known what she was going to say, but there had never been any question that she would rally around afterward. After all, Marcy was all she had. "I don't think I'll change," Marcy said. "I'll just wear what I've got on."

"You look very sweet. We can just go ahead and leave now, then, if you're ready."

When Marcy thought of Mrs. Lancaster, at least, she felt a deep glow of satisfaction. She had fought back. She had not allowed herself to be meekly shorn like some helpless lamb. She had shrieked her protest to the whole world.

Of course, it would have been nice to be going someplace with Sam and Luke after graduation instead of going over to Aunt Hilda's, but she couldn't expect that. Things were going to be a little delicate for a while, maybe. Luke would support her, but after all he did live at home and might have to keep a low profile just at first. It might be hard for him to call or come see her for a while. And Sam was so ridiculously protective of Pip. As if he weren't perfectly well able to take care of himself! Look at the steamroller job he and his family had done on her, snatching the prize of valedictorian from her teeth at the very last minute! Marcy was not sorry for what she had done, but too much adrenaline had been pumping through her system all day for her to feel completely at her ease. She was conscious of having taken on powerful enemies, and she was uneasy about what their next move would be. Distractedly, she looked around for her pocketbook.

"Ready?" asked her mother.

Sam and Luke parked behind Wendy's to eat their burgers. "You think you know people," Luke said as he snapped the top off his Frostie. "You think the two of you are on the same wavelength, and then something like this happens." He stabbed the milk shake with a spoon. "I'm starting to think I don't know anybody. The world is a zoo, that's all. You never know what's going to hit you in the face next. Oh, no, look!" He slumped down in the seat in a vain attempt to hide.

Sam, startled, looked around. All she saw was a plump middle-aged man walking toward them across the parking lot.

"It's Mr. Maxwell," Luke growled.

"Mr. Maxwell?"

"From the newspaper. Jeez, he sees that we've seen him. There's no way we can get away now. Oh, great, this is just what I need."

Coming up to them, Mr. Maxwell smiled affably and bent down to talk into Luke's window. "This is a piece of luck. I tried your house a couple of times but the line was always busy. Do you think your mother would like to make a statement to the *Banner*?"

"I don't think so, Mr. Maxwell. She was so surprised, you know. She wouldn't know what to say except there's nothing in the accusations. But maybe you'd better ask her."

Mr. Maxwell rubbed his hands together. "It was just pure luck that I happened to be at the graduation.

Bernice, my brother's girl, was graduating today, so we all turned out. I tell you though, that salutatory speech went by so fast, that by the time I realized I had a story, I barely had time to get my notebook out of my pocket.'' He produced a small spiral-bound notebook. ''Could you just spell the salutatorian's name for me, Luke?''

''M-A-R-C-Y M-C-N-A-I-R,'' said Luke woodenly.

''McNair. You're sure that's right, now? Good. Luckily, my brother got the whole thing on tape. He just bought a new video outfit last week. Now, I hear your mother's going to make a statement to the school board. That right?''

''You'll have to ask her.''

''We'll cover the school board meeting, of course. We always do. Well, I guess I'll keep trying to reach your mother on the phone. I can see you don't want to speak for her, and I can understand that. Good seeing you, Luke.''

Luke shot a venomous look at Mr. Maxwell's retreating back. ''Ghoul,'' he snarled.

Sam's parents got in late from the dinner party that night, but Sam was still up. She had been keyed up all evening, expecting to hear from Pip or Marcy. But the phone refused to ring.

''How was the party?'' she asked.

Sam's mother rolled her eyes. ''Guess what the chief entertainment of the evening was?''

''Slides of the Fergusons' vacation?''

''Worse. A videotape of the graduation.''

''You've got to be kidding!''

"I wish I were. Fourteen people to dinner and most of them had not been fortunate enough to be eyewitnesses. There was an amazing amount of interest, wouldn't you say, Larry?"

"Everyone was agog. Let's face it, the whole town is talking about what happened. Practically everyone there had already heard about it, but the videotape was seen as a special treat."

"Your father was asked to give his professional opinion."

"I told them that stuff about Eloise was a bunch of hooey, of course. A teacher of the highest reputation, I said. She's widely thought to be one of the best teachers in the system."

"Marcy came in for a lot of sympathy, it seemed to me."

"Naturally. Well, here is a poor kid, for all practical purposes abandoned by her father, working all through high school to help her mother make ends meet and still keeping her grades up. I can't help but sympathize with her myself, even after what she's done. After all, this is a kid I've seen grow up. One who's been in and out of our house since she was just a little thing."

"What about Pip?" asked Sam anxiously. "Did anybody say anything about Pip?"

"I had to explain about the weighting of the grades and that business of the grades being transferred from the private school. A little blame to pass around there. Maybe there should be some more firm policy about how these things are handled. Not that I think for a minute there was any wrongdoing. It's just a question of avoiding the appearance of any favoritism and also a question of all the kids knowing exactly where they stand."

"Pip thinks everybody's going to be against him because his family is rich."

"I wouldn't know about that. Once we explained that he was our daughter's steady boyfriend—"

"And really a very nice boy, too," her mother put in.

"That sort of put the kibosh on any negative remarks people might have been inclined to make."

"I don't think people would be likely to blame, Pip, anyway, Sam. They'd be more likely to fault his father. It's no secret that Phil Byron has enough ambition to fuel a battleship. I suppose there are some who think he might be willing to exert some sort of pressure to further his ambitions for Pip. How far they think he'd go is another question. But there's certainly no possibility, in our mind, of his bribing Eloise Lancaster. The idea's absurd. We tried to make that clear."

"Everybody always blames the parents," commented Sam's dad. "People tonight were saying that Marcy's mom must have pushed her so hard she cracked. As if anybody could push a kid to make good grades! If pushing a kid would get you good grades, Luke would have been the valedictorian, not Pip. People are a mass of prejudices."

Sam was not interested in other people's problems just then. "Pip is sure everybody's prejudiced against him," she said anxiously.

"He may be right," sighed her father. "After all, most people have just heard Marcy's side of the story."

Chapter Ten

I understand what you're saying, Pip, and I don't like it any better than you do that the Rotary Scholarship is coming to you, but don't you see that she's put us in a position where we can't do anything about it?'' Phillip Byron's hands were clasped behind his back, and he was staring sightlessly at the book-lined wall in his study at home.

"Maybe we could make it up to her some other way. Weren't you talking about creating a company scholarship fund? Why couldn't Marcy be the first recipient?''

"Not a chance. What you don't seem to grasp is that the newspaper is covering this whole affair. And once my campaign gets into full swing, both the newspaper people and the opposition are going to be looking for any sort of dirt on me. Anything we did to help this girl out now would look like an admission of guilt on my part that would be sure to come out later."

"But just on compassionate grounds—"

"Don't you believe for a minute that would fly. When you read of some politician saying he only gave money to somebody on compassionate grounds, what do you think? That it was a payoff, pure and simple, that's what you think. I feel as sorry for the girl as you do, Pip, but by accusing us the way she has, she's tied our hands."

Pip perched on the corner of his father's desk. "I hate to snatch the bread right out of her mouth, that's all. It makes me feel like the bloated capitalist in some communist cartoon."

His father threw his hands in the air in a helpless gesture. "What can we do? The company lawyer's going to issue a statement Monday about the procedure used to choose the recipients of the education awards. You and I know he'll be speaking the truth. I just hope other people can recognize it. All we can do is sit tight and hope for the best."

"Sam tells me that Luke's mother is going to make a statement at the school board meeting."

"Our lawyer will read our statement at that meeting, too. But what we're hoping is that this will die down with a minimum of press coverage, so the less you or I say, the better. A lawyer standing up there reading a statement doesn't make good copy. I'm afraid you and I do. We simply have to stay out of it. Does Sam have any idea whether Marcy is going to make a statement?"

Pip fiddled with a pen. "She's already made her statement, hasn't she? Anyway, Sam wouldn't know.

I don't think she's talked to Marcy since it happened."

At the Morrisons', Sam's mother was just hanging up the phone. "That was Eloise," she told Sam, her forehead puckering. "She wanted to know if we've heard from Luke. It seems he's just taken off. He left a note saying he'd be away for a while. I think that's what bothered Eloise as much as anything. She says it's so unlike Luke to leave a note. She thought it seemed almost sinister."

"I guess he just needed to get away," said Sam. She threw herself heavily into a kitchen chair. "Nothing strange about that. I can kind of see how he feels. He doesn't need to report to work until the first, and there's nothing but gloom and doom around his house. I sympathize. Probably he just left town for a few days looking for a little fun."

"Alone?"

"What do you mean?"

Her mother coughed. "I think Eloise is wondering if Marcy is with him."

"She's got it all wrong, Mom. Luke is furious with Marcy. He hasn't spoken to her since it happened."

"Eloise doesn't seem to be as sure of that as you are. She wants to know if Marcy has left town, but, of course, she can hardly call up there herself to ask, under the circumstances."

"You mean she's still got this bug about how they might be running away to get married? She is so out of touch. And I guess she wants *me* to call Marcy?"

"I think that's what she's hoping, yes. I said I'd call her back if I could find out anything."

Sam sighed. "Actually, calling Marcy isn't such a bad idea. I guess I'm going to have to talk to her sometime. And talking to her over the phone I won't be tempted to kill her the way I would be if I saw her in person. But what am I going to say? 'Well, Marce, just wanted to check in on how you're getting along since you did your best to ruin Pip's life.' Great. Well, if I've got to call her, I think I'd better do it from my room. It's going to be kind of tricky to figure out what to say."

Sam practiced several opening remarks on her way up the stairs, but when she got up to the room and actually got through to Marcy, her voice seemed to give out. It looked for a moment as if Marcy might conclude she was one of those weird callers who just breathe heavily into the receiver. At last Sam managed a weak, "Uh, hi, how are you?"

"Sam! Gee, it's great to hear from you. I was starting to think you were mad at me. Have you talked to Luke? I figured he might find it a little difficult to call me, but I was hoping he could slip away sometime to come over. But I haven't seen him."

Sam fastened on the one fact at hand, the one she could deal with. "You don't know where Luke is, either? He seems to have disappeared."

"Disappeared!" Marcy gasped.

"Not disappeared as in a missing person, Marcy. He left a note saying he'd be away for a while."

"He never said anything to me about it. Why would he want to go away without saying a word?"

Sam choked. She hardly knew where to begin. How could it be that Marcy could seem so unaware of the effects of what she had done? "He's—he's a little perturbed with you, Marce. Did you expect him to sit there and cheer while you told the whole town his mother was a criminal?''

"I didn't say anything that wasn't true."

Sam groaned. "Marcy, you are so wrong, wrong, wrong. You said things up there that you don't have a shred of proof for."

"I just laid out the facts and let people draw their own conclusions. I can see how Luke might be a little bit annoyed but—"

"Marcy, you said his mother had been paid off. His *mother*!"

"Don't give me that, Sam. You know Luke doesn't have any use for his mother. The relationship is purely technical."

"Marcy, I'm going to say this slowly in words of two syllables. Now listen—the woman is his mother. Think about that and all it means. And while you're at it, think about what you did to poor Pip."

"I didn't expect you to be on my side," Marcy said in a quavering voice. "It's pretty clear who counts with you."

"Oh, Marcy," Sam wailed. But Marcy had hung up.

Sam dragged herself downstairs to report to her mother. "Luke is not with Marcy. She doesn't know where he is. She hasn't heard from him."

"How did she seem, Sam?"

"She hung up on me."

Thursday night Sam attended the school board meeting with her parents. "We have to be there to give Eloise some moral support," her father said.

Other people had had the same idea. Several organizations to which Luke's mother belonged had shown up en masse, in addition to a large number of her fellow teachers and, of course, a reporter from the *Banner*.

"Luke's still not back," said Sam's mother, as they filed into their seats. "I certainly thought he would be back for this meeting."

"Probably forgot when it was," said Sam's dad. "Face it. Reliability's never been his strong suit."

"Shh."

The superintendent of schools rose and explained that the school board was allowing certain people to make statements on matters they were concerned about, that the school board did not intend to take any action on these questions, but was merely offering the meeting as a public forum on this occasion.

Then a representative of the firm of Brown, Dunlop and Pearsall rose and read a dry statement on the methods used for selecting the Byron Tobacco Education Awards recipients. "I would like to stress," he concluded, "that although Mr. Phillip Byron made the public presentation of the awards, he at no time had a hand in the selection of the recipients." As the lawyer sat down, the overhead lights gleamed on his balding head.

Then Luke's mother rose to read her statement.

"I have taught Latin and senior English classes at Lee for ten years and have been responsible for the Advanced Placement English course for three years. The Advanced Placement English course is the equivalent of a freshman course at college and has far more stringent requirements than a high-school English class. This is why when Marcy McNair asked to have another teacher read her senior thesis, I felt unable to agree to it. Marcy's paper was a good paper, a sound paper, but not up to the best standards of Advanced Placement English. In my professional opinion, it did not merit an A. I did not at that time realize the impact a B would have on Marcy's grade average, but had I realized it, my judgment would have been the same. I cannot allow the student's ambitions to influence my grading procedures.

Unhappy with the B I gave her, Marcy then asked to see my grade book. I could not violate the privacy of my other students and let her see it. A student has the right to see his own grades, but not the grades of others. I have been quite consistent in my stand on grades being kept private, and to deviate from it to satisfy one disgruntled student would have been quite unprofessional.

"Marcy accused me of having favorites. I do have a favorite student—" She paused and smiled a little sadly, "—my son, Luke. But when he took Latin from me, he made an even lower grade than Marcy. I do not believe that I have ever allowed my personal feelings about students to influence my grading. Nor have I ever been offered a bribe to improve a student's grade. That these unfounded accusations were made is deeply painful for me and for my family. I can never forget that a day of celebration for over a thousand seniors and their families was turned into an opportunity to air a private grievance in what amounted to a perversion of Lee's graduation ceremony.''

Luke's mother sat down. The superintendent rose to thank everyone for their remarks. "Can we leave now?" Sam whispered to her mother. Her mother nodded briefly, and together with several rows of other observers they filed out before the regular business of the meeting began.

When they reached their car outside, Sam's algebra teacher waved from the next car. "Came off pretty well, don't you think?" he called.

"I thought so, too," Sam's dad said.

They all got into the car. "I did think Eloise's speech came across very well, didn't you, Ginny?"

"Oh, yes. Clear, simple, to the point. We'll have to call the Lancasters when we get home and tell her so."

Sam looked at the moon over the agricultural building. It had surfaced briefly from behind heavy clouds. "I just wonder where Luke can be," she said anxiously. "I certainly thought he would be here."

The next day was the day of Happy's graduation party. Rain threatened all day. The sky was heavy and dark and seemed to press warmly down against the earth. Sam rather regretted that she had decided at the last minute to go shopping for a new dress for the party. As she hurried into the shop, she wished she had at least thought to bring an umbrella.

In the dressing room of Reischauer's Sam pulled a dress over her head in some haste. She wanted to finish her shopping and get home before the storm broke. As she zipped herself up she heard voices in the next dressing room.

"What's a thousand dollars to the Byrons? Nothing. Have you seen that car Pip drives? I bet it cost $15,000. I really feel sorry for Marcy. Everybody knew she was supposed to be the valedictorian, and it looks pretty suspicious to me. I don't blame her for thinking things weren't on the up and up."

Sam strained to hear, trying to recognize the voices. She was sure they were people she knew; she just couldn't quite place them.

"Do you think he's going to be there tonight?"

"Pip? Sure he is. He's going to face it out. I just saw Sam come in looking for a dress."

"You did? Where? Here?"

Suddenly the voices sunk to a whisper. Sam glanced at herself in the mirror. The dress fit. It looked fine. She was going to buy it and get out of this place before she heard any more people slandering Pip.

As she carried the big paper bag emblazoned Reischauer's to her car, Sam despairingly wondered how long people were going to talk about Marcy's speech. The statement Mrs. Lancaster made at the school board didn't seem to have put a damper on the talk at all. She wondered if a report on it in the evening paper would help or whether Marcy's speech had stirred up a muddy welter of ill feeling that would never recede.

The air felt hot and oppressive. If only it weren't so damp, Sam thought. It would almost be a relief for the rain to come. Get it over with.

But the rain held off all day though the sky grew ever blacker. The heavy clouds hung low until late afternoon. Only when Pip drove up to Sam's house to pick her up for the party did a cool breeze at last appear, hinting at the approach of rain. As Pip opened the door for Sam, he cast a glance up at the sky. "It's going to be coming down any minute. Hurry up and get on in."

Sam lifted up her skirt and slid into the car.

"Do you think Marcy's going to be at the party?" he asked her.

"She was invited." Sam looked at him anxiously. "We don't have to go, Pip, if you think it will be awkward."

"I do have to go, Sam. Didn't you know? If I didn't, it would look like an admission of guilt, according to my father. I'm supposed to be going around exhibiting my clear conscience every chance I get. What do you bet when we go in everybody turns around and stares at me?"

Sam lifted her chin. "If they stare it'll just be because we're such a striking couple."

Pip got in behind the wheel. "I'll bet people all over town are talking about nothing else," he said grimly.

"Oh, no, I don't think so. It's already blowing over," she lied.

Chapter Eleven

The parking lot at the Silver Lake Restaurant was packed. It always was on a Friday night. Months before, the Chambers family had taken the precaution of reserving the entire ballroom for Happy's party.

Sam saw any number of kids she knew getting out of cars. When she got out herself, a fat cold drop of rain fell on her head.

"Here it comes," said Pip. He produced a large black umbrella from the car, and they hurried inside.

"The Chambers's party?" asked the woman with the professional smile. "Right this way. To the ballroom."

When they stepped into the ballroom, Sam at once smelled cooking shrimp. At a long white table near her, a man in a white chef's hat was sautéing scallops in a copper skillet.

Happy appeared, wearing a dress of ivory crepe that showed her dark hair and pale skin to advantage. "Sam! Pip! I'm so glad you could come. Mother, you remember Pip, don't you?"

Happy's eyes were glittering so that Sam had the uneasy feeling she should check her seams to see if anything had come undone. Then it occurred to her that possibly all Happy had ever wanted was to be the center of attention. Perhaps this party fulfilled all her desires and the glitter in her eyes was from simple happiness. Mrs. Chambers, a grayer version of Happy, smiled graciously at Sam.

As Happy and her mother turned to greet new arrivals, Sam looked around and saw that floodlights on the deck outside the big glass windows that fronted on the lake illuminated a spectacular fall of rain. The raindrops were molten silver where they fell close to the light. On the dimmer reaches of the deck, rain puddled on deck chairs and streamed off furled beach umbrellas. And beyond the deck was the darkness of the lake. The rain was falling so heavily now she could not make out the small light that usually burned at the end of the dock.

To the left of the big windows Sam spotted a familiar figure standing at the oyster bar. She clutched Pip's arm. "It's Luke! He's back."

She pulled Pip over there. "Luke! Where have you been?"

Luke flushed. "Keep it down, Sam, will you?"

"I was really starting to get worried. What can you have been doing all this time? You even missed the school board meeting!"

"I'm, uh, just going to go over and get some of those scallops," said Pip hastily. "You want any, Sam?"

When Pip had left, Luke bent his head close to Sam's and muttered, "I drove over to the mountains."

"You took a vacation?" She looked at him blankly.

"Not exactly."

Her heart sank. "You haven't been doing anything illegal, have you, Luke?"

"Nah." His ears reddened. "I went over to look at some colleges."

"Colleges!"

"Would you keep your voice down, Sam? Have a heart. Everybody's looking at us."

Sam glanced around. Everybody she could see was busy stuffing their face with raw oysters, but she obediently lowered her voice. "I don't think I quite follow you," she said.

"I started thinking about how Marcy had added everything up and came to the one hundred percent wrong conclusion, like you said, and then I started saying to myself, who am I to think I'm any smarter, you know? Maybe I ought to give college a whirl for a semester or two and see what it's like."

"Have you told your mother?"

Luke popped an oyster in his mouth. "Nope. I just got back. I guess I'll tell her when I get in tonight. There's a place over there where you just take one course at a time, you see, kind of intensive study and then when you finish it you go on to the next. It's not the regular old semester system. And meanwhile you work to help pay your expenses. I looked at a couple of two-year schools over near Asheville, too, but I liked this other place best. Mostly, the jobs are around the school. Working in the cafeteria, that kind of thing. But I talked to the admissions guy, and it looks like I might be able to manage something working as a kind of intern in a paper in town. That way, I'd have it both ways, you see. I wouldn't have to take much money from my folks, I'd get some experience and I'd still, well, do this college thing, too."

"That sounds like a good idea to me." It sounded to her like a propitiation gift to his mother, but she didn't think it would be a good idea to point that out. It couldn't do Luke any harm to try college, and it would certainly do his mother good. The poor woman was due for a break. "Is Marcy here?"

Luke shrugged. Suddenly Marcy appeared, flanked by Reggie and Yolanda, who showed every sign of being oyster addicts. They were bearing directly toward the oyster bar with determination. Luke looked Marcy full in the face and abruptly turned his back on her. He pushed his way into the crowd and disappeared. Marcy looked as if she had been slapped. Smudges of pink stood out on her cheekbones emphasizing the pallor of the skin below the blush-on.

Sam smiled weakly at her and looked around for Pip. She didn't want him to have to face running into Marcy by himself. Finally she spotted him over by the canopied bar where the scallops were being sautéed, and she swiftly made her way over there. A band began to play, and Happy's father led Happy onto the floor. After a moment several other couples joined them.

"So what's Luke up to?" Pip asked her, spearing a scallop with his fork. "Smuggling hash over mountain passes?"

"He's going to college. He's very embarrassed about it."

Pip smiled. "Figures. He hates to ruin a perfect record. Do you want to dance?"

Sam let him lead her into the middle of the room where now six or eight couples were dancing. "Poor Marcy," she murmured. "I think it's finally hitting her what she's done. Luke just cut her dead."

"Would you do me a favor and not say 'poor Marcy' more than every five minutes? It seems to me that 'poor Pip' makes more sense."

"Pip! Look! She's going outside!"

Pip's head snapped around. Marcy was blindly groping her way out the glass door and onto the deck. The lights shone on her a minute and then she disappeared into the darkness.

"You think she's going to jump in?" asked Pip in alarm.

Sam's hand was raised to her mouth. "I don't know."

"Okay, hang on," he said grimly. "I'm going after her."

A hundred curious eyes followed Pip as he rushed out onto the deck and disappeared into the darkness and rain.

Sam felt a hand on her shoulder and jumped a mile. "What's going on?" Luke asked.

The rain hit Pip in the face the minute he stepped out the door. By the time he had cautiously made his way along the wet and slippery deck to the beginning of the dock, his feet were beginning to squish in his shoes, rain was dripping off his nose and matting his hair. He wiped a hand over his eyes and moved cautiously out onto the dock. The problem was that if anybody fell in the lake when it was dark like this, he wasn't sure you could see to find them. He wished he had thought to ask Sam if Marcy could swim. That was a pretty basic question, after all.

At least he was pretty sure she had gone out on the dock. There was in fact no other way off the deck that he could see except back through the ballroom. When he had walked a ways out on the dock, he spotted a dark shape at the end. She was out there all right. He could just make out that someone was sitting there next to the light. He was afraid if he called out, she might jump in. Luckily, the rain was making so much racket she wouldn't be able to hear his footsteps. Cursing the instincts that led him to rush to the rescue, he made his way out to her, hoping that she wasn't going to get a mind to push him in. Nothing she did would surprise him at this point.

He was almost up to her before she heard him and looked around. She was sitting with her legs dangling off the dock and her hair was in her face. The light was too poor and the rain too heavy for him to tell much else.

"What did you come out here for?" she yelled at him. She sounded strange, but he realized at once that it was only that she was crying. She had probably never intended to jump in the lake after all.

"Why did you follow me?" she demanded.

"God only knows," he said, wishing he hadn't. His cuffs were sodden, his pants were soaked and it was only a matter of moments until his jacket was wet through as well. A fine sight he would look going back into the party. He felt like a blinking idiot.

"I guess you're going to tell me what a rotten person I am," she said in a nasty tone.

"You expect me to give you a medal?" Pip had to raise his voice a little to be heard over the rain. "You were all wrong about what you said, you know. My father never paid off Mrs. Lancaster. He didn't have anything to do with who got those awards. If you thought about it a minute, you'd realize that. How could he even know who you had for English?"

"Well, obviously I was going to be in AP English. Anybody could figure that out."

"Marcy, you don't think I needed to be valedictorian, right?"

"Well, you didn't, did you? You've got everything else. You don't need the money. You don't need the recognition."

"Okay, if you're right about that, and I don't need it, then why would my father go to the risk of bribing some teacher for me to get it? Think about it!"

"You're going to deny that they fiddled your grades when you transferred in?"

"No, I'm not going to deny it. There wasn't any secret about it. We talked to the school people about it, and everybody agreed it seemed like the fair thing to do at the time."

"Nobody asked me. I think it stank."

"Marcy!" Luke yelled.

Pip looked around to see a figure vaguely silhouetted against the floodlights jogging toward them.

Marcy pushed her dark hair out of her eyes. "I'm awfully popular all of a sudden. I thought you weren't speaking to me."

"Well, I had to come out to make sure he wasn't pushing you into the lake, didn't I?" yelled Luke.

"Well, he wasn't."

"Maybe I should, then."

"I'm a very strong swimmer," she said defiantly.

Pip was soaked to the skin. His shoes, he realized were ruined. Worse, he had made a spectacle of himself. What was he doing standing here in the rain with these two? Let them kill each other. Good riddance. Gritting his teeth, he left them arguing at the end of the dock and made his sodden way back to the lighted deck. He would have liked to shake his fists at the sky and yell. That would have given the people inside something to stare at for sure and might have relieved his feelings a little, but a lifetime's habit of self-control was too strong to break. As he got up to the deck, he saw that Sam was standing under the floodlights holding his big black umbrella over her.

"Everything all right?" she called.

"Everything's just super. Your idiot friend is out there arguing with her idiot boyfriend and I'm soaking wet." It hardly made sense to get under the umbrella, he was so wet already, but he did it anyway. At least the rain wasn't dripping down the back of his neck that way, and he could feel the heat of Sam's body next to his. He shivered and looked back at the ballroom. Clusters of people were standing near the windows looking out at them. He wished they would go away and eat scallops or something.

"I think we can get out through the kitchen over this way," Sam said.

They picked their way past the deck chairs to a screened door where they were met by a blast of heat. Sam furled the umbrella, took Pip's hand and led him through the kitchen, murmuring "Excuse me, excuse me," over and over again to the bemused kitchen staff. A moment later they were standing outside in the rain next to some garbage cans.

"Home?" suggested Sam.

Pip groaned. "Definitely."

When they got to the car, Pip stripped off his jacket and shirt, and dropped them on the floor of the back seat. Sam handed him a handkerchief, and he rubbed his head with it, drying off his hair as best he could.

"So what were you and Marcy saying out there?"

"I told her she was wrong about my father paying off Mrs. Lancaster, and she called me a liar."

"Oh, no! Did she really?"

"Well, not in exactly those words, but that was the flavor of it, all right." Pip wiped the handkerchief across his wet face and then dropped it, too, onto the floor of the back seat. Rain was drumming down on the thin roof of the convertible. "Why," he groaned, "did I have to go after her? Now everybody will have even more to talk about. Did you see them pressing their noses up against the glass, staring at us? Next, people will be saying that I tried to kill her. That's what Luke said. He said he thought I was going to push her in! I ask you. Why did I have to go out there?"

Sam patted him on the knee. "You went after her because you are a really good person, that's why."

"Jeez, what a stinking party!"

"Let's just go someplace and get burgers."

Pip pulled off his shoes and socks and with a fastidious grimace dropped them behind him. "It'll have to be someplace with a drive-in window. I'm not decent."

Sam smiled. "You look good to me."

Pip patted his pants pocket and a momentary look of panic went over his face only to disappear at once when he found what he was looking for. He produced a small rounded blue-velvet box. "I didn't exactly plan it this way, Sam. But then nothing has gone the way I planned." He bent his head over it and cautiously flipped the box open. Sam could see the glimmer of a dark stone ringed with diamonds.

"You can wear it on any finger you want, I guess," he said grudgingly. "It doesn't have to be an engagement ring. But don't go hocking it. It's a sapphire."

Sam slipped it on her left ring finger. "I love you, Pip," she said softly. "And that's a promise."

He bent to kiss her. "Okay," he said in a satisfied voice. "At least this part is going the way I planned."

Luke, less concerned than Pip with causing a scene and too mad to care, took Marcy by the hand and dragged her back into the ballroom. They dripped on the floor and attracted flabbergasted stares as he tugged her toward the door. Mrs. Chambers looked at them in horror as they passed her. "It was a lovely party, Mrs. Chambers," Marcy stuttered. "Thank you for having us."

Luke jerked her through the door to the ballroom, and moments later they were out in his car. "You didn't bring your car, did you?"

"I came with Reggie and Yolanda."

"In there are all the raw oysters and shrimp I can eat," said Luke, "and I'm out here in this car with nothing but a bunch of old gum wrappings. I suppose you realize this is all your fault? What did you have to go wading out into the storm for? Is this some kind of death wish or some long latent exhibitionistic tendency of yours or something, or is it just some deep dark plot to make sure I am as miserable as is humanly possible? You want to explain it to me?"

Marcy folded her arms and shivered. "I was upset."

"Could you have been upset because it hit you what an utter idiot you are and how you did your best to ruin my mother's career and her reputation if not her health and sanity, is that it? I swear, I actually have been feeling sorry for Pip. I never thought I'd live to see the day, but when you go after somebody, Marcy, you don't just fool around. No, you call 'em a liar and a cheat in front of everybody they'll ever know and make sure it gets in the newspaper. Next we'll have satellite coverage. You're practically ruining the lives of everybody who ever cared about you. Is that what's getting you down, sweetie pie?"

"I guess so."

"You guess so! Give me strength, Lord. If you aren't the craziest, most vindictive, most destructively ambitious, most blind woman in the world, I'd hate to see who comes in first."

"All of those things," sniffled Marcy. "It's true."

"If you start crying, I swear I'm going to punch you. You have given me enough grief to last a lifetime, and I don't need any more, believe me. It's bad enough that I'm going to have to go to college."

Marcy's eyes widened.

"And don't start congratulating yourself about that. You have absolutely nothing to congratulate yourself about. You are the lowest of the low."

"It's true."

"My mother returns the extra pennies when people give her too much change, for Pete's sake. She's the last person in the world to do anything dishonest."

"I might have gotten the wrong idea."

"Jeez, don't do me any favors. *Might* have gotten the wrong idea. You were wrong, dead wrong. Didn't you think to talk to anybody about it before you went off half-cocked?"

"I thought anybody I told would try to stop me."

"Well, you're right about that. Jerusalem. I'd have handcuffed you to the car if I'd have known what was up." Luke heaved a heavy sigh. "You know, my mother's a good woman in a lot of ways but she's not very quick to forgive."

"Unlike you."

"Oh, you can do anything to me. I put up with it all, right? Kick me around, lie about my family, soak me to the skin, starve me to death and I come running back for more. I'm pretty stupid." He started the engine. "I guess from now on I'm going to have to see you in secret," he said gloomily.

"You will? See me, I mean?"

"I never did have any sense."

"Carolina is really a good school," Marcy said breathlessly. "Very strong in the liberal arts. I'm thinking of asking Sam if she would room with me. Do you think she would?"

"Well, I would." He smiled. "I guess it's remotely possible Sam might be that dumb, too. So what do we do now?"

Marcy squeezed some water out of her hair. "Let's try to find one of those places that has a hand blow dryer in the bathroom, okay? I need to stand under one for about an hour."

Luke's car splashed through a puddle at the parking lot exit and pulled out onto the road. The headlights beamed into the rain and converged ahead.

"We're friends, then?" Marcy asked hesitantly.

"I guess so, may heaven preserve me. Hey, I think that's Byron's car!" The white Mercedes ahead of them weaved a little. "He ought to pay more attention to what he's doing," said Luke sternly.

"Sam must be distracting him."

"Must be." Luke blew his horn and passed the Mercedes.

Pip answered with five brief syncopated blasts of his horn.

"He sounds happy," said Marcy.

"Maybe so. Jeez, what a crazy world." As the car turned toward town Marcy realized that Luke was unconsciously humming the tune to "Hail, Hail, the Gang's All Here."

For the first time in weeks she smiled.

* * * * *

A series of novels
for the sophisticated
young adult—like you!

——◆——◆——◆——

Keepsake is . . .
fantastic
dynamic
terrific
. . . but most of all ROMANTIC

——◆——◆——◆——

Don't miss out, pick up your copy
where books are sold.

2 to choose from each month!

Keepsake

—books designed for today's sophisticated young reader—like you!

Two new books filled with romance, mystery, unforgettable experiences and interesting characters available each month.

Pick up your copy wherever books are sold.

COMING NEXT MONTH
FROM
Keepsake

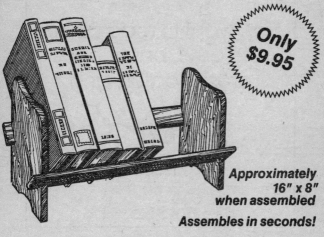